A Secret Encounter

AMISH SECRETS
~ BOOK 2 ~

J. E. B. Spredemann

Blessed Publishing

BOOKS BY J.E.B. SPREDEMANN (*J. Spredemann)

Available Now:

AMISH GIRLS SERIES (for teens)

Joanna's Struggle

Danika's Journey

Chloe's Revelation

Susanna's Surprise

Annie's Decision

Abigail's Triumph

Brooke's Quest

NOVELLAS

*Amish by Accident**

An Unforgivable Secret (AMISH SECRETS SERIES)*

A Secret Encounter (AMISH SECRETS SERIES)*

Coming Soon:

AMISH GIRLS SERIES

Leah's Legacy – February 2014

NOVELLAS

*Learning to Love – Saul's Story** – Spring 2014

A Secret of the Heart(AMISH SECRETS SERIES)* – Summer-Fall 2014

To Joshua and Jessica…

Two of the most compassionate people
I've had the privilege to know

Author's Note

It should be noted that the Amish people and their communities differ one from another. There are, in fact, no two Amish communities exactly alike. It is this premise on which this book is written. We have taken cautious steps to assure the authenticity of Amish practices and customs. Both Old Order Amish and New Order Amish are portrayed in this work of fiction and may be inconsistent with some Amish communities.

We, as *Englischers,* can learn a lot from the Plain People and their simple way of life. Their hard work, close-knit family life, and concern for others are to be applauded. As the Lord wills, may this special culture continue to be respected and remain so for many centuries to come, and may God's light of salvation reach their hearts.

Characters in A Secret Encounter

Joseph (Joe) Bender – Protagonist

Harvey (Harv) – Joe's friend

Anna Smucker – Protagonist

Mammi – Anna's grandmother

Aaron Gingerich – Anna's beau

Linda – Anna's employer, proprietor of Threads of Beauty

Jacob Schrock – Anna's cousin

Rachel Schrock – Jacob's wife

Samuel Beachy – Joe's friend

Judah Hostettler – Bishop of several Amish church districts

Jonathan Fisher – Minister

Unofficial Glossary
of Pennsylvania Dutch Words

Ab im kopp – Crazy

Ach – Oh

Aentie – Aunt

Aldi – Girlfriend

Alt maedel – Old maid

Ausbund – Amish hymn book

Bann – Excommunication from Amish church

Boppli – Baby

Bopplin – Babies

Brieder - Brothers

Bruder – Brother

Bu - Boy

Dat, Daed – Dad

(Gross)Dawdi – Grandfather

Demut – Humility

Denki – Thanks

Der Herr – The Lord

Dummkopp – Dummy

Englischer – A non-Amish person

Ferhoodled – Mixed up, Crazy

Fraa – Woman, Wife

Geh – Go

Gott – God

Grossmudder – Grandmother

Gut – Good

Haus – House

Hiya – Hi

Hochmut – Pride

Ich liebe dich – I love you

Jah – Yes

Kapp – Prayer Covering

Kind – Child

Kinner – Children

Kinskinner – Grandchildren

Kumm – Come

Lieb – Love

Liewi – Dear

Maed – Girls

Maedel – Girl

Mamm – Mom

Mammi – Grandmother

Maut – Maid

Mei Lieb – My Love

Mein Klein Bopp – My little doll

Mein Liewe – My Dear

Mudder – Mother

Nee – No

Ordnung – Rules of the Amish community

Rumspringa – Running around years

Schatzi – Honey

Schtupp – Living room

Sohn – Son

Vadder – Father

Verboten – Forbidden

Vorsinger – Song leader

Wilkom – Welcome

Wunderbaar – Wonderful

PROLOGUE

*J*oseph Bender hung his head, contemplating the implications of his actions. *Am I really shunned?* By the disappointed countenances of his family, he realized it to be true. What would he do now? Where would he go? His father's words played in his mind for the umpteenth time, "You are no longer my son. Leave at once. There is no room in this home for unrepentant sinners."

Joseph heaved a sigh of defeat. He searched his mother's face for some trace of compassion, but she could only look away as she blinked at the tears that trailed her weathered appearance. So desperately he wanted to reach his arms around his mother and embrace her one last time, but he knew the time for affection had passed. It expired the moment Bishop Burkholder read his sentence.

He threw an old duffel bag over his shoulder. It contained the few belongings he owned: two pairs of trousers, two long sleeve cotton shirts, a few undergarments, and socks. He donned his black coat that had seen better days and his straw hat, and walked out of his folks' home, and out of their lives, forever.

In just a few short months, he'd lost everything he'd ever held dear...

ONE

*A*nna Smucker finished putting the dishes in the cup-board just minutes before the kitchen timer buzzed. "*Ach*, I'm running late again, *Mammi*. Would you mind preparing something for supper tonight?" Her eyes pleaded.

"*Liewi*, I wished you didn't have to run off every day." *Mammi* shook her head.

"But you know we need the money. Sellin' eggs ain't enough to keep this farm running. If we could just get more tourists in here to buy up your quilts...*ach*, listen to me prattling on when I got a job to get to!" She shook her head.

"Of course, I'll fix somethin' up for us. Don't you worry none." Her kind grandmother patted her hand gently. "Now, *geh*."

"*Denki, Mammi.*" Anna leaned over and placed a kiss on *Mammi*'s cheek. "Love you, *Mammi*. Have a *gut* day."

Anna hurried out to her buggy. Thank goodness she'd had the forethought to hitch Brazen up early today. It seemed lately she couldn't wake early enough to tend to all the chores around the place. There was so much that needed to be done, and she wasn't about to leave the work for *Mammi* to tend to.

It had been a year since her father passed on to Glory. She'd never realized how much he did around the farm until he was gone. Knowing now what it took to keep the farm running, she wished she could go back and tell her father thank you for the countless hours he'd labored on their behalf.

As of last month, she'd sold off the last of the cattle. Now she and *Mammi* no longer received income from their milk. But after paying off their debts, the money they received from the sale was only enough to keep up with their mortgage payments until the end of the year.

Why, oh why, had her father mortgaged their land? She knew for a fact that *Grossdawdi* had left a tidy sum when he died. It would have been plenty to pay their debt in full. But instead, her adventurous father had ambitiously purchased five hundred head of cattle. The cows weren't necessarily a bad idea, but they weren't counting on her father passing away so quickly. He had yet to turn a profit.

When Anna approached other Amish ranchers in the community, none were able – or willing – to purchase the cattle. Apparently her father had been swindled. At least that's what the *Englischer* said that graciously took the bovine off her hands. He claimed he was giving her a deal, paying even more than they were worth. Perhaps it was true. *Dat* had always dreamed of owning a cattle ranch. She was certain he wasn't the first overzealous dreamer willing to pay whatever it took for a dream to become a reality. If only *Dat* hadn't passed on...

Anna flicked the reins, hoping Brazen would get her to work on time. Although her boss knew about the situation at home and was sympathetic to her plight, she knew she wouldn't be happy if she was late again. She had been kind enough to allow *Mammi* to sell her quilts in her fabric shop, although it seemed there weren't too many tourists in their neck of the woods. She'd heard that quilts similar to her *grossmudder*'s sold for over a thousand dollars in some places where the tourist trade was rampant. Imagine that! But *Mammi*'s only went for a few hundred dollars; such a shame considering the quality work that she put into them.

But at least Anna had this job. That was something she could be thankful for. She always tried to look on the positive side of things. After all, there was not much she could do to change their circumstances. She would be grateful for the blessings they did have, because she'd always heard that there were countless others out there that had far less than she. Yes, *Gott* had been good to them.

"Anna, go ahead and take your lunch break now," her boss called from behind the register.

"All right," Anna answered back, retrieving her purse and coat from the break room.

Linda's eyes brightened as she nodded toward the front of the store. "Someone's here for you, Anna."

Anna poked her head around the corner. It was Aaron. He had shown interest in her for a year now, and just two months ago she'd accepted his offer to court her. They never had much chance to spend a lot of time together because they were both so busy – he with his dog-breeding business, and she with work and farm chores. Occasionally he would show up out of the blue and take her to lunch, which she thought was a nice gesture.

"Hi, Aaron. In town for somethin' special today?" she asked, raising an eyebrow.

"Nah, not really. Just had to pick up a few things for *Dat* at the hardware store." He shrugged. "Ready to go?"

"*Jah*, I'll let Linda know," Anna said.

"Where would you like to go today?" Aaron asked, his handsome gray eyes sparkled.

She shrugged. "Pizza?"

"Pizza sounds great to me." He grasped her small hand and led the way down the block.

"Joseph! Joseph!" Joe startled out of an already fitful sleep. He lifted his head, glancing around the abandoned alley. No one was there. Had he truly heard a voice, or was his subconscious playing tricks on him again? *No one's called me Joseph in years. Not since...*

He pulled the newspapers up over his body and around his neck in an attempt to keep the chill out. His tattered coat kept some of the elements out, but the gaping holes seemed to welcome every miniscule draft. Laying his head once again on the plastic grocery bag that held his old shirt, his eyelids drifted shut.

Joe was just on the verge of nocturnal ecstasy when the blasted voice called to him again. *For Pete's sake, can't a man get a few minutes of sleep?* He scowled inwardly. He raised his head again, but this time his mind was keenly aware of the body hovering over him.

"You need somethin' Harvey?" Of course, he already knew the answer.

"Yeah, Joe. You got a smoke? I need one real bad." His hands shook, evidencing the truth of the man's words.

Grudgingly, Joe reached into his pants pocket and handed over a cigarette. "You really need to get your own and stop bummin' off of others."

"I know, I know. Just this one last time," the older man said, lighting the end of his cancer stick. That's what Joseph's grandfather used to call cigarettes.

"You said that last time. The last ten times actually," Joe stated wryly.

Harvey took a puff and offered it to Joe. He shook his head, rejecting his offer. "Tryin' to quit," he explained.

"Really, Joe? Then can I have —"

"No. You may not have the rest of my pack," Joe answered, rising from his corner in the alley.

"Hey, where ya goin' man?" Harvey called to him.

"Just stretchin' my legs a bit. I'll be back."

"Can I use your papers while you're gone?" the older man pleaded, holding up the rumpled mass of yesteryear's news.

"Sure," Joe stated, walking toward one of the main streets. Looking back at his shivering friend, he decided to turn back around. "Hey, man. Why don't you take my coat too? I'll be walkin' so I'll be plenty warm."

"Thanks, Joe. 'Preciate that."

Joe rubbed his hands together to try to create a little friction. Boy was the air nippy today. He picked up his pace and strolled down the sidewalk, noticing the diverse displays in the shop windows. It seemed Christmas was upon them again. *Another year alone*, Joe thought bitterly. It had always been extremely difficult to keep thoughts of his childhood at bay this time of year.

He remembered how *Mamm*'s face would brighten when he'd bring in the pine boughs from outside. She used to decorate the house up right perty, he'd thought. And although their Christmases were always plain and simple, they had been special. He recalled a time when... *Enough of that!* He chided himself. *This* was his reality now. No matter how much he missed home, going back wasn't an option. And never would be.

The wind picked up and a chill seeped through the holes in the back of his shirt where the seams wore thin. *Mamm* had been a *gut* seamstress, but even the best couldn't sew seams to withstand several years of daily wear. He ducked into one of the nearby establishments. He hadn't even the opportunity to warm himself before a not-so gentleman asked him to leave before he was given a police escort off the property.

As he stepped back out into the cold, he couldn't help but notice that the other people on the sidewalk gave him wide berth. Some even went so far as to walk in the street to avoid him. He wasn't surprised by the lack of sympathy the strangers possessed. After all, his family couldn't stand the sight of him either.

If they could only see him now. His hair had naturally formed dreadlocks, hanging past his shoulders – a shame for sure and for certain. Because he'd lost so much weight, his worn trousers were now held up with an old bungee cord he'd found on the street. A sorry replacement for the suspenders he was used to wearing – those had busted last year. Harv had offered him some denim trousers that were in a little better shape, but they never felt right. His beard had grown to his chest, scraggly as ever. Back home, only married men were allowed to wear face whiskers. *Married,* he mused. Now that was a circumstance he'd never have to dwell on. He'd spent plenty of time thinking of what could've been, what *should've* been…

A blast of muddy rain water brought him back to the present once again. Couldn't drivers be a little more considerate of folks walkin' along the sidewalk? Now, he was not only cold, but wet too. And dirty. Not that he was exactly clean before he'd been sprayed with the gush of water. He didn't remember the last time he'd taken a decent bath. Once in a while though, he would sneak into a fast food restaurant and use the restroom to freshen up a bit. No wonder people veered as far out of his path as possible, he probably reeked like a skunk. Or worse.

Aaron and Anna made their way back toward the fabric shop. Anna's lunch break was nearly over. She now held a Styrofoam box of leftover pizza in one hand, still warm.

"Watch out," Aaron warned. "Here comes another beggar."

Walking the opposite direction was a homeless man. By the look of him, she thought him to be in his early thirties. *What would make one so young live on the streets?*

As the man neared, she noticed his filthy clothing and couldn't deny the offensive odor the hapless man emanated. Aaron pulled her arm to lead her far out of his path, but compassion took over. She looked down at the box of leftover pizza and knew what she must do. As she started to speak, Aaron halted her.

"Don't give that to him. He'll probably sell it for drugs," he whispered loud enough that she was sure the destitute man had overheard.

Embarrassed by her beau's judgmental assumptions, she attempted to hand the box to the man with a look of apology. Aaron's hand grabbed the box and tossed it to the man, or more accurately, to the ground. Anna abruptly scowled at Aaron and bent down to pick up the box for the man.

"I'm sorry." She handed the box to the stranger, her eyes apologetic. She couldn't believe Aaron's rudeness.

The man gratefully took the box and for a second, coddled it like a newborn *boppli*. Realizing his treasure, he immediately opened it, stuffing half a slice of the delicious goodness into his mouth. He nodded his thanks and sauntered off toward a nearby alley.

"What'd you do that for?" Aaron scolded.

Beside herself, Anna was simply at a loss for words. "Do what?" she asked between gritted teeth.

"You gave that…that vagrant our food after I told you not to! You disobeyed me." He huffed.

"I – I *disobeyed* you?" she asked indignantly. She knew a woman's place was to follow the man, but this seemed a little ridiculous. Besides, they weren't married.

"How can I protect you when you won't heed my warnings? That man could have been dangerous," he clumsily explained his actions.

"He didn't look dangerous to me. He just looked hungry. We're supposed to feed the hungry, *jah*?"

Aaron sighed. "I guess you have a point. But I don't think it's a *gut* idea for you to be talking to homeless *Englischers*."

She looked up and noticed they had arrived at her workplace.

"See ya at meetin' on Sunday?" his voice softened a spell.

"*Jah, Mammi* and I should be there," Anna said, glad he was leaving now.

Aaron waved a hand and started toward his buggy.

"Here Harvey, ya gotta try this!" Joe excitedly offered his older friend a slice of pizza.

His companion bit into the cheesy delicacy. "Mmm...I ain't had nothin' this good in a long time. Ya didn't steal it, did ya?"

"I may be a lot of things, Harv, but a thief I am not," Joe assured his old buddy.

"Where'd ya get it from then?" He sank his chops into another bite.

"A kind woman," he simply stated.

"Must've been an angel," Harv mused aloud.

Joe's eyebrows rose. He remembered the Amish woman's rosy cheeks and kind smile. "Perhaps."

"Well, I hope you told her thank you," Harvey said.

Did I tell her thank you? "I don't think I did. Maybe I'll see her again someday and I can tell her then." The thought brought a smile to Joe's lips.

TWO

*A*nna sat at the dinner table with *Mammi*. She couldn't help but think of the homeless man right now. Here, she and her grandmother had more than enough for the two of them. She blew on her chicken vegetable soup and shivered as she thought of how the poor man practically scarfed down the pizza she'd given him. *What would it be like to go hungry for days on end?*

Her attention was stolen away by a clap of thunder outside. *Mammi* moved toward the window, peering out into the dreary night. A bright flicker from outside illuminated the entire kitchen. *How is that man doing right now? Does he have a place to stay dry?* Anna couldn't recall whether the man wore a jacket or not, but she couldn't forget his trousers. As he'd walked away, she noticed a gaping hole on the backside exposing his bare skin underneath. She immediately looked away feeling embarrassed for the man. Yet the pants appeared homemade. Had someone from her community given them to him?

It seemed that no matter what she did that evening, her thoughts were consumed with the misfortunate homeless man. She'd tried to occupy her mind with knitting, but as the warm scarf took form in her nimble hands, she pictured herself offering it to the cold stranger. When she read the Word of God before bedtime, she couldn't get around the fact that Jesus ministered to the poor and needy. As she laid her head on her soft pillow to sleep, she couldn't help but wonder what the stranger lay his head on, this miserably chilly night. Surely he hadn't a warm quilt to wrap around his body. These were her last thoughts as she drifted off to sleep...

Another clap of thunder and Anna shot straight up. She took the flashlight from her bureau and shined it on the small wind-up clock that sat atop her nightstand. Three o'clock. Had it stormed the whole night through? She forced herself out of her cozy bed and made her way to the bathroom, the cold wooden floor seeping through her socks.

She and *Mammi* both shared the large house, but the upstairs was exclusively hers. *Mammi* had said she was too old to be trudging up the stairs day and night, but Anna knew in truth she preferred the bottom floor. After all, she slept in the room she and *Grossdawdi* occupied when they were first wed.

What was it like to be newly wed? Anna often wondered. At twenty-two years of age, she was nearly considered an *alt maedel* in her community. She supposed she should be thankful that Aaron had shown an interest in her. But for some reason, she couldn't picture a future with him no matter how hard she tried.

Warmth filled her soul when she thought of the dream she'd had last night. It had been strange indeed. *She had been ever so happy. Anna had just removed a casserole from the oven when a small girl of about three bounced through the door, her blonde braids hanging freely about her shoulders. "Mama, Mama!" she'd said. "Dat just got some new kittens!" she chattered in their native Pennsylvania German dialect.*

"Oh, really?" Anna's bright smile stretched across her face.

A tall bearded man clambered through the door now with a kitten in each hand. "That's right!" he'd said, bending down to kiss her cheek. He handed her one of the small fluffy creatures. "One for mein klein bopp *and one for my* lieb.*"*

Anna placed a hand over her warm cheek now, as though his kiss lingered there. She pinned up her long hair and glanced at a small hand mirror to make sure no blonde strands had escaped. The dream had felt so real. She closed her eyes, attempting to picture the sweet gentle man in her dreams. But it seemed his face was always just out of focus. However, the smile in his voice and his kindness toward her was impeccably clear.

She sighed. Would there only be a man for her in her dreams, or did he really exist somewhere out there? One thing she was certain of, though. The man in her dream was *not* Aaron Gingerich.

Anna smiled as though she held the key to a long-lost treasure chest. Time had seemed to tick by so slowly today. Twelve o'clock had finally rolled around and she couldn't wait to deliver the extra sandwich she'd made to the homeless man.

Now she walked down the sidewalk toward the alley. A seed of doubt had been planted in her mind, and with it, fear. What if Aaron was right? What if the man was violent – dangerous? Should she really be traipsing out here all alone? *I'll just peek around the corner*, she told herself. *I can leave the food by the alley so he can see it, and then I can walk away.*

Anna discreetly looked into the alley. To her disappointment, and a smidgen of relief, she had to admit, the man was not there. In fact, the place seemed conspicuously deserted. She heard a rustling near the large metal trash receptacle and a cat jumped out, startling her so badly she'd almost wet her pants, or more accurately, her dress. She heard another noise and an eerie chill up her spine sent her scurrying back in the direction of the fabric shop.

Halfway there, she glanced down at the bag in her hand. *What am I going to do with this now? If I leave it there, surely the cats will eat it.* Anna shrugged her shoulders in resignation and turned back around. After all, she didn't need another sandwich and she knew Linda had already eaten. If she took it home, *Mammi* would start asking questions that she was certain she didn't want to answer. So why not leave it for the cats to enjoy?

After gingerly setting the bag down on the ground at the entrance to the alley, Anna again set back toward the shop. Why did she feel as though she was committing some heinous crime and she had to sneak around? *I'm feeding the needy, for crying out loud!*

"She's gone; you can come out from hiding now," Harvey stated. "What's with you anyway, Joe?"

Joe shrugged. "Well, she's Amish, that's all."

"And? Do you have an aversion to Amish people or somethin'?" Harv lifted a brow. "Or perhaps it's just God in general?"

Joe quickly changed the subject, eagerly rubbing his hands together. "So, what do you think she left us?"

"You, Joe. She left it for you. She ain't even seen me yet," Harvey stated emphatically. "And if she did, I might've scared her away." He chuckled, rubbing his long gray beard reminiscent of jolly ole St. Nick.

Joe emerged from their spot near some old upturned wooden crates and quickly retrieved the brown paper bag near the alley entrance. He didn't open the bag until he was back in his spot. He delved into the bag and smiled. "I was right!" His eyes lit up.

Harvey grinned at him in eager anticipation, rubbing his hands together. "Well, what's in the bag?"

"Cookies! Just like *Mamm* used to pack for my lunch when I was a *kind*." His grin couldn't get any wider as he pulled one out of a napkin. "Look at this, Harvey! Even a whoopie pie! This one's mine. But I'll let you have a bite too."

"Are ya tellin' me you're Amish?" Harvey's face darkened.

"Mm...hmm," Joseph mumbled around a mouthful of whoopie pie, rolling his eyes in pure ecstasy.

"Well, that explains a whole lot." He slapped Joseph on the back.

"What do ya mean?" Joseph asked, licking the creamy filling off his bottom lip.

"Why you're so nice for one thing. I ain't never met a mean Amish person," Harvey stated authoritatively.

"Harv, how many Amish folk you know?" Joseph raised an eyebrow, genuinely curious.

"You." He smiled.

Joseph bellowed.

"Well, don't go laughin' at me yet. That young woman was Amish and she seems real nice. I think that counts for two."

You didn't meet her boyfriend, he thought wryly. *Or Bishop Burkholder.* But he chose not to dwell on the past. Not right now. Not when he was just given a wonderful-*gut* gift that was only half eaten now. "Care for half a sandwich?" He held out the generously packed homemade hoagie roll.

"Sure." Harv smiled, taking his portion. "Ya know. Since you're Amish and all, maybe you should get to know that woman," the older man suggested.

Joseph laughed, holding up both hands in protest. "Oh no. Don't even start thinkin' like that. Besides, I *used* to be Amish. I'm not anymore."

A scraggly alley cat approached Joseph, meowing as she rubbed against his ankle. He reached down and stroked the pathetic feline. "You hungry? Here, go ahead and have some of my sandwich." He tore off a quarter of his portion and set it on the ground for the cat, which devoured every crumb.

"I mean it, Joe. You deserve yourself a good woman," Harv continued.

"No, I don't," Joe snapped back. The last thing he deserved was a *gut* woman. Besides, a woman like that would never give him the time of day.

THREE

Jeremiah Gingerich leaned back against the cushion and eyed his son from his wooden chair in the *schtupp*. He'd been pretending to read *The Budget*, but his distracting thoughts weighed heavily. Aaron was the youngest *bu* in the family and at the age of twenty four, he had yet to marry. The last thing he desired was for his son to end up an old bachelor.

He gazed out the window, the last few rays of sunshine fought for their place in the clouds. Brilliant hues of pink, purple, and orange dazzled the evening sky. Why wasn't Aaron with his *aldi*? *Maed* love nights like this – at least Tabitha had. He remembered the countless times they'd watched the sunset walking hand in hand by the creek or cuddled together in his courting buggy.

"Aaron, *Sohn*, you know I really want ya to have this farm. But ya need to get yourself hitched first," Aaron's father said.

"I'm workin' on it, *Dat*," Aaron uttered between gritted teeth. The problem was, he didn't think he and Anna were anywhere near the marrying stage in their courtship. Maybe he should step things up a bit.

"Well, if you know what ya want, you gotta go after it," his father suggested. "Ya ain't getting' any younger."

"I think I just might do that, *Daed.*" Aaron pulled his hat off the rack and placed it on his head. He grunted inwardly, loathing when his father threw his age at him, which was often. It wasn't as though he hadn't heard the story a hundred times, *I was married with four* kinner *by the time I was your age.*

Didn't his father realize he was aware of his own marital status? It's not like he hadn't courted any *maed.* There'd just never been one that seemed truly interested in him...or should he say none that interested *him.* He was fully cognizant of his good looks and fine physique, not that he was *hochmut* or anything. But by the way the *maed* behaved around him, their attraction was apparent. He tried not to let it go to his head but at the same time, he knew he could probably attract any girl he wanted.

And he decided he wanted Anna. After all, she was the most beautiful girl in these parts. A chill shot up his back when he thought of the time he'd driven up in his buggy and she was hanging up the laundry. Ever so gently the wind had picked up causing her cape dress to outline her voluptuous figure. He'd never forget that image. Yes, he had every intention of making Anna his *fraa.*

Aaron knew what he would do. Surely a sweet puppy would melt any girl's heart. He took purposeful strides toward the barn. Stepping into the dark dwelling, he quickly lit the lantern that hung on a nail by the door. Soon his eyes adjusted to the dim lighting.

He quickly walked over to the barricaded area where the Blue Tick Hound pups were caged. He spotted his favorite immediately and scooped him up into his arms. He stroked the frisky puppy as it licked his fingers ferociously, eyeing its brown and black coloring. For sure this pup was the most desirable out of the lot and would most definitely fetch the best price, with his distinct markings and what not.

But he knew only the best would do for Anna. Besides, if he played his cards right, the puppy would end up being his anyway. Not a bad thing to have the offspring of champion hunting dogs, for a hunting Amish man. Aaron smirked at his own genius.

Anna had a busy day at work and couldn't wait to just finish the rest of the chores and put her feet up. It seemed Amish and *Englisch* alike had intentions of giving handmade items for Christmas this year. She supposed business would probably increase even more between now and the holiday. A yawn escaped her lips as she closed the barn door and headed back toward the house.

Her thoughts drifted again to the lunches she'd been leaving near the alley every day. Since that day with Aaron, she still hadn't seen a trace of the homeless man. She hoped Aaron hadn't scared him off, but perhaps that is why he remained aloof. *Does everybody treat destitute folk as if they hold no value? Surely God values them.*

Each time she left food, it disappeared, so apparently *some-one* was enjoying the meals. Somehow, though, she wished she could do more. Bring the man a blanket maybe? Or clothes? She was certain some of *Dat*'s old trousers and shirts sat in a box up in the attic. She'd meant to give it away after he and *Mamm* passed, but never found an opportune time. Until now. But surely he wouldn't fit into her father's things. Her father had been stocky, while this man appeared quite thin. She supposed she could alter the trousers by guesstimating the man's size. Yes, that's what she would do.

"*Mammi*, do we still have that box of *Dat*'s things up in the attic?" Anna asked, stepping into the front sitting room.

Mammi pushed her glasses atop her nose farther, setting her crochet project on her lap. "I haven't moved it. So, I guess if you haven't moved it either then it's probably still there. Did ya need somethin' out of it?"

Anna shrugged noncommittally. "I just thought maybe we should give some of it away since we aren't using it."

"*Jah*, that is a *gut* idea." She nodded satisfactorily and turned her attention back to her afghan.

Good. Now Anna didn't have to worry about *Mammi* asking questions while she rummaged through the attic. Now, she just hoped there were no spiders lurking up there. Mice, she could deal with. But there was nothing worse than the feel of a potentially poisonous arachnid crawling around on one's skin. Anna shivered just thinking about it.

As Anna topped the last step to the attic, she heard the unmistakable sound of horse hooves and a buggy rolling to a stop in their yard. She sighed, partly in relief of not having to fend off the spiders for an extra few moments. But now she'd have to postpone her lofty excursion for another time.

"Anna," her grandmother called up the stairs. "It looks like Aaron's buggy. You'd better come down."

Anna groaned. "Coming."

Aaron held the puppy behind his back as he knocked on the Smuckers' back door for the second time. The creature was beginning to get restless. *Why hasn't she opened the door yet?* he wondered impatiently.

When the door opened, he said the first thing that came to his mind. "It's about time."

Anna's eyes widened. "Excuse me?"

"*Ach*, I'm sorry, it's just that...here." He handed her the puppy.

Anna received the puppy with a puzzled look on her face. "Uh, he's cute. This is a nice dog, Aaron." She handed the dog back.

"*Nee.* It's for you. I wanted you to have him as a pet," he explained.

"Oh. Uh...thank you, Aaron. But it's not really the best time for us to be takin' in a pup. We don't have any extra resources and I'm afraid a dog would require quite a bit of food. And with me working at the fabric shop and my chores, I'm afraid I wouldn't have any time to spend with it," she said, hoping she didn't hurt his feelings.

"So you really don't want him?" he asked with surprise.

She shook her head. "We can't take him. I'm sorry, Aaron."

Out of all the reactions he thought he might get, this one had never crossed Aaron's mind. *I guess I'll take him back home.* Aaron looked back to his buggy, wondering whether the puppy would stay in the box while he spent time with Anna.

"Would ya go on a short walk with me? I'll just put the puppy up in my buggy," Aaron said.

"*Jah,* just a short walk." Anna really didn't want to, but she already felt guilty about rejecting his gift. It wasn't like Aaron to bring gifts and she wondered if maybe he was up to something. But what could it be?

They walked along her property and Anna listened politely as Aaron talked all about his puppy business. While he continued on, she began wondering why she was still seeing him. He was handsome, *jah,* but it seemed as though they didn't really mesh well together. Their interests were so different and, besides their faith, she couldn't think of one thing they had in common. No, she needed someone who valued the same things she valued. Someone compassionate, who wouldn't turn their back on another in need.

When they arrived back at the small front porch, Aaron took her hand. "Uh, Anna, I wanted to ask you something."

Anna's eyes bulged as Aaron came closer and pressed his lips – and his body – against hers. She stood frozen like a statue and stiffened her lips as she pushed him away. This was not how she'd envisioned her first kiss.

"What's wrong? Can't I even get a kiss from my girl?" he asked, forcing her close. He bent down to kiss her again, holding her tight. She squirmed under his strong grip and he released her, letting out a chuckle. "Just relax, would ya? I was wanting to ask you to marry me."

Definitely not! "*Nee,* Aaron. I don't think we're meant to be together," she said, taking a step toward the house.

"What do you mean, Anna? I bring you a nice pup and you reject it. I court you for months and *now* you're not interested?" His voice raised.

"I'm sorry, Aaron, but–"

"No, Anna. I cannot accept that," he interrupted. "Please, will you just consider it? Listen, I'm sorry for trying to steal a kiss from you."

"Aaron, please. You and I are just too different. We wouldn't make a good couple," Anna attempted to explain without totally offending him. "I wouldn't make a *gut fraa* for you."

"You'd make a fine *fraa,* Anna. I know, I've tasted your cooking. And I've been inside your home for meeting; it appeared clean enough." Aaron gently stroked her forearm.

Anna sighed. *Surely he knows there's more to marriage than a clean house and food on the table!*

"Anna, please give me another chance. Let's give it another month or two so we can get to know each other better," he coaxed.

"All right." She gave in. "Another month."

"*Denki*, Anna. You'll see. We'll make a *gut* couple," Aaron assured her.

A squeal from the buggy brought Anna the relief she sought. "Uh...I think your pup is getting antsy."

"*Jah*, I'd better get him home. I'll be seeing ya soon," he said, tipping his hat before hopping into the carriage.

A yawn escaped Anna's lips as she entered her and *Mammi*'s quiet home. Only a single lamp burned on the small coffee table in the sitting room, indicating that *Mammi* had already gone to bed. Forgetting about her previous quest for clothing, she readied herself for bed and slipped into another dream-filled night.

FOUR

"What are we going to do, Joe?" Harvey eyed his friend over a bite of the warm soup Anna had left in the alley earlier. The two of them had watched from behind the dumpster as she'd carefully poured the soup from a Thermos into a large disposable plastic bowl.

Joseph's eyebrows knit together. "What are you talking about? You can't just ask a question like that without explaining to a body what you're talking about."

"You know, the woman. We can't just let her keep bringing us food every day."

Joe nodded. "You're right. I'll talk to her and tell her to stop."

"Well, wait now. That's not what I meant. Don't you think we should say something to her? I mean, we should at least let her know we appreciate what she's doing," Harvey reasoned.

Joseph tugged on his beard, thinking. "You've got a point. All right, I'll take care of it. But you've got to be gone when she comes by tomorrow, cause I ain't talkin' to her in front of you."

"Okay. Okay. Hey Joe, do you think you can ask her to bring more of them whoopie pies? Or some more of that hot cocoa? Or how about—"

"Harv," Joseph said in a warning tone.

"All right. Maybe just mention that we liked them?" Harvey pleaded.

Joseph laughed, shaking his head. "You are too much, old friend."

Anna sang in her quiet soprano voice as she mucked out Brazen's stall. The horse whinnied in approval when she mentioned the Saviour's name. Anna looked up in amazement, wondering if perhaps the animals had their own special way of communicating with God.

After shoveling the dung into the wheel barrel, she added fresh hay and water to Brazen's trough, then led the horse back in. She treated Brazen to an apple for behaving nicely and rubbed the horse's head affectionately.

Anna's shoulders ached from all the extra work she'd been doing around the farm. *It would be great to have a man around to do all this,* she mused. If she'd had extra money she would have hired someone immediately after *Dat* died. *Maybe I can get Aaron to come over and do some of the work around here.* She suddenly remembered the other evening and thought better of it, *then again, that might not be the best idea.* Anna released a frustrated breath.

Pray. The word seemed to float above her as though it were a wishy flower gracefully meandering on a gentle spring breeze, just waiting for her to catch it. She reached out and grabbed it, carefully examined it, and then released it back into the air. *Lord, please send an answer to our problem, according to Thy will. Amen.*

Mammi's glowing countenance greeted Anna as she trudged through the door. Anna stood a little taller in anticipation of whatever news had brought such excitement to her grandmother.

"You're not going to guess what came in the mail today!" *Mammi* held out a letter to Anna. "Your cousin Jacob Schrock and his *fraa* Rachel are coming to visit us next week! Isn't that *wunderbaar*?"

Anna smiled broadly, skimming over the letter. "*Ach, jah.* That's great. How long will they be staying?"

Mammi snatched the letter back. "I'm not sure. I don't think they mentioned how long they'd stay. But won't it be *wunderbaar* to have someone to visit with? I can't wait to see how big the *kinner* are now. And I'm sure Jacob will help with the outdoor chores."

Tears pricked Anna's eyes. "Oh *Mammi*, I just prayed for help. I didn't expect the answer so soon. *Gott* sure is *gut, jah*?"

"The Lord heareth the prayer of the righteous..." *Mammi* placed her weathered hand over Anna's and smiled. "Yes, my dear Anna. *Gott* is always *gut*."

Anna placed a bolt of green fabric back into its place among the other similar hues. She loved how all the colors were displayed as though they were a beautiful rainbow. It seemed green and red fabrics were selling more and more often now that fall was in full swing.

She glanced over at the customers examining *Mammi's* Christmas quilt, hoping they wouldn't have to discount the price. *Mammi* did such fine work; the quilt was easily worth the four hundred dollars they were asking for it. When the customers left without buying anything, Anna frowned in disappointment. *If only we had more tourists,* Anna thought.

She'd been to the larger, more popular towns where the Amish tourist trade flourished. In fact, she'd even taken some of their handmade goods to the farmers' market and mud sales on occasion. But that had been when her folks were still alive. She'd never be able to do it now; it was simply too much for one person to manage. Not to mention she wouldn't feel comfortable driving all that way, especially in the wee hours of the morning prior to the sun peeking over the eastern horizon.

"Anna, would you mind taking this delivery over to Mrs. Lapp at the candle shop? I've been meaning to do it all morning but I've barely had time to breathe. I still have that order of crocheted mittens and scarves that need to be completed too," Linda said.

"No problem. I'll take it right now, if you'd like," Anna offered.

"Oh, thank you, Anna. You're a Godsend."

Anna clutched the bag of ribbon at her side as she walked toward Nature's Candle, several blocks away from Threads of Beauty. Anna smiled thinking how befitting the name of her employer's shop was. Not only because the store sold beautiful things, but also because Linda's name meant beautiful.

As Anna stepped into the candle shop, sweet fragrances immediately enveloped her senses. Oh, how she wished she could afford to buy a candle in every scent she desired. That would be nice, but it wasn't practical and it would be silly to spend her hard-earned money on something that wasn't an absolute necessity. She didn't begrudge handing over her money to pay the bills, she just thought that it would be nice to buy something luxurious once in a while.

After delivering the promised goods to Faith and pocketing the money, she took one last whiff of a large vanilla candle displayed near the front window. She peeked at the bottom to see the price and almost dropped it when she discovered what it cost. No, she wouldn't be buying that candle anytime soon. Who had forty dollars to spend on a candle that would burn up in just a few weeks?

The streets seemed surprisingly quiet for the middle of the day. Anna passed by a couple of local shops and one of the few fast food places in town. The greasy smell made her stomach queasy and she wondered how people could eat at those places all the time.

A firm grasp on her upper arm caught Anna completely off guard as she was being pulled behind a building. She would have screamed but for the large hand that covered her mouth. Her heart beat rapidly as she squirmed under the stranger's firm hold.

"Shh...I'm not going to hurt you. I'm the man you gave the pizza to. I'll take my hand away from your mouth if you promise not to scream," he said calmly.

Aaron's words echoed in her head once again, cautioning her about the homeless man. Anna wriggled, trying to break loose of his grip, then gave up when she realized her efforts were fruitless.

Joseph chuckled at her futile attempts. "Promise not to scream?" he asked again. "I swear I won't hurt you."

Anna nodded and the man quickly uncovered her mouth, as promised. "You shouldn't swear. Will you please let me go now?" she asked, her back still pinned against his chest.

He gently released his hold on her and she spun around. "What did you do that for? You scared me half to death," she said.

"I didn't want to frighten you. I guess it didn't work." He shrugged.

"Have you ever thought about the direct approach? You know...Hello, my name is...what's your name?"

"Joe."

She continued, "Hello, my name is Joe. Do you mind if I speak with you for a few minutes?"

Joseph guffawed.

Anna gasped and placed a hand on her hip. "I don't think this is funny. You could have given me a heart attack, you know!" She tried to suppress a smile that threatened.

"I know. I'm sorry. Please accept my sincerest apology." He bowed at the waist.

Anna giggled. "Apology accepted."

Joseph cordially held out his hand. "Hello, Miss. My name is Joe. Do you mind if I speak with you a few minutes?"

Anna played along and shook his hand, then thought about Linda waiting for her at the fabric shop and grimaced. "I'm sorry, I can't. I really need to get back to work. Linda will be sending out a search party if I'm not back soon."

"Oh, uh, okay," he said disappointedly.

"How about if I meet you in the alley at lunch time?" she suggested.

Joseph smiled. "That sounds great."

"So, did ya meet her, Joe? What did she say, huh?" Harvey asked eagerly.

"Settle down, Harv. She's way too young for you," Joseph teased.

"Maybe...maybe not." He shrugged.

Joseph gawked at his friend as though he were...well... *ferhoodled.*

"Relax, bud. I was just joshing ya." Harvey grinned. "So, what's she like?"

"Oh Harv, she's amazing." Joseph closed his eyes, recalling their brief conversation.

"I knew it! I knew someone as kind as that would be perfect for you," Harvey emphatically proclaimed.

"No, Harvey. She deserves someone much better than me. A *gut* Amish man with a job and a farm, someone that can provide for all her wants and needs and give her children. Not me. I have nothing to give her."

"Hey man, you ever hear of livin' on love?"

"Oh yes, I can see it now. 'Come here, my sweet wife. How do you like our cozy little corner of the alley? Would you like me to scrounge through the garbage to find you more newspapers to keep you warm?' I think not, Harv." Joseph shook his head in discouragement.

Anna couldn't wait for lunchtime to roll around. She didn't know why, but for some reason she felt comfortable with the homeless man. As though she could identify with him somehow. Who would've thought the two of them would hit it off so well? Certainly not her.

Why was it that she'd thought she'd be so different from him? Had she considered the homeless man, Joe, inferior to herself? It was almost as though she hadn't considered him to be a genuine person prior to meeting him. *How's that for* demut? She thought shamefully.

Lord, please forgive me. Help me to be more like You. Help me to shine Your love through my life.

"Do you hear that, Joe? It's footsteps. She's coming. I think she's coming!" Harvey said excitedly.

"Calm down, old friend. I'll go check it out." Joseph arose from his crate behind the dumpster and set his playing cards face down. "No cheating," he warned. "And stay there until I say."

"All right, all right."

Joseph hurriedly walked toward the opening of the alley. He arrived just as Anna was rounding the corner, causing her to jump.

"*Ach,* Joe. You've got to stop doing that," Anna said, placing a hand over her heart.

"Sorry, uh..." Joseph realized he hadn't caught her name.

"Anna. My name is Anna," she said. "So, is this your home?" She leaned slightly to the right, craning her neck around his shoulder to observe the quiet alleyway.

"Yep, this is it. Home sweet home," he said sarcastically. "Would you like a tour?"

Anna smiled. "Sure, just as long as nothing's going to jump out at me."

"Just stick close to me and you'll be fine." Joseph led the way down the alley, feeling a bit awkward. *This is no place for a woman*, he thought disgracefully.

Anna quietly followed Joe, taking in her surroundings. For the most part, the alleyway was empty. Water trickled out from a pipe that apparently came from the back of one of the brick buildings, leaving a grayish-green stain on the wall behind it. Anna shuddered wondering if that's where Joe got his drinking water from. Aside from a few large dumpsters, there appeared to be nothing on this back street. *How can someone live here?*

As they neared the second dumpster, Joseph turned to Anna and spoke up. "Anna, there's someone I'd like you to meet."

Anna nodded.

"Okay, Harv. You may come out now," he called.

Anna grinned as an older fellow with a cigarette hanging between his smiling lips popped out from behind the dumpster. His gray hair and beard reminded Anna of *Grossdawdi* Schrock, *mamm's vadder*, who'd passed on to Glory about ten years ago. She immediately felt an instant kinship with the older man.

"Well, well. Look what we've got here. You're right, Joe. She sure is a perty little thing." Harvey's words caused Anna to blush. "Ah, and humble, too."

Joseph spoke up, attempting to save Anna from further embarrassment. "Harvey, this is Anna. Anna, Harvey," he introduced.

"Pleased to make your acquaintance, fair lady," Harv said, removing his hat and dipping his head.

"*Gut* to meet you too, Harvey," Anna said, enjoying the old man's antics.

Joseph frowned at Harvey and a look passed between the two of them.

"I'm sorry, Joe. I couldn't help it. I was nervous about meeting the girl," Harvey explained, then turned to Anna. "Joe's upset 'cause I took one of his smokes."

Anna eyed them both, choosing to change the subject to avoid conflict. "So, where do you eat? I've got lunch here if anyone's hungry." She smiled.

"Now there's a girl after my own heart," Harv said. "Come with me, fair lady, and I will accompany you to our humble dining room." Harvey held out his elbow.

Anna glanced at Joe who shrugged with a smile, then looped her arm in Harvey's elbow. Harvey escorted Anna around the large dumpster to where two large wooden crates stood upright forming a small table. Two other crates were turned upside down on each side of the table and Harvey offered Anna a seat on one of them.

"You may sit here, fair lady. And Joe and I will share the other. It ain't too often we get to entertain guests."

Anna eyed the crate warily, hesitant to sit down just yet. "There are no spiders under that, are there?"

Joseph promptly picked up the crate and examined the inside. "Ah...just a couple of black widows and a few daddy longlegs."

Anna's jaw dropped and her eyes widened in horror.

"Just kidding, just kidding," Joe held up his hands in surrender, laughing all the while.

"*Ach*, you are terrible!" Anna playfully punched his arm.

"Hey, I thought the Amish were supposed to be nonviolent," Joseph said, rubbing the place she'd hit him as though it hurt.

"Okay, you two, enough fighting. I don't know about y'all, but I'm ready to eat my lunch. What did our fair lady bring for us today?" Harvey eyed the small insulated chest Anna had set on the make-shift table. Joe sent him a disapproving look.

A smile brightened Anna's face as they sat down. She and *Mammi* lived simply, *jah*, but they seemed fancy compared to her present company. "Let's see." She removed a container from the box and both men licked their lips in anticipation. "This is meatloaf. There are mashed potatoes in this one. And some green beans in this." She set everything out and opened the lids, and then pulled out a half loaf of bread as well.

Harvey's eyes sparkled in addition to his silly grin. "Can I marry you?"

Anna chuckled.

Joseph kicked Harvey under the table and he let out a yelp.

"Hey, Joe, what'd ya do that for? I was just kidding," Harvey said.

"Mind your manners, we got a lady here," he warned, then turned to Anna. "Thank you for this, Anna. We really do appreciate it and all the other things you've been bringing us. You are very kind."

Anna caught the sincerity in his eyes and felt heat rise to her cheeks. "No need to thank me. I'm just doing my Christian duty. If you want to thank someone, thank God. He's the one that laid you on my heart," she deflected.

"Ah yes, but *you* are the willing servant," he maintained.

"Shall we eat?" Harvey spoke up unabashedly.

"Yes," Anna agreed, handing each man a paper plate and fork. "Joe, would you like to say the blessing?"

Joseph's face reddened. "No, thank you."

"I will say grace," Harv volunteered. "Let us bow our heads. Oh, gracious Heavenly Father above, we thank thee for this fine woman – Ow, come on, Joe," Harvey grimaced and rubbed his leg where Joe had kicked him under the table again, then continued the prayer. "...Who has so unselfishly provided food for our nourishment. May you bless her and this food. Amen." Harvey turned to Joseph. "What'd I say this time?"

"I'll tell ya later," Joe said.

"Well, until then I'm going to have to stand up or buy some heavily insulated steel-toed boots to wear when Miss Anna comes to visit," Harv said.

Anna attempted to conceal a smile as she held out the meatloaf for the men to partake of first. She was certain this was the most interesting lunch she'd ever enjoyed.

FIVE

*U*nsure of the time, Anna hurried back to the fabric shop. *I hope I'm not late,* she chided herself for not having paid attention to the time. Opening the door to the shop, she glanced up at the clock. *Two minutes till one.* Anna sighed in relief.

She looked around the shop, but there was no trace of Linda. *She's probably in the back.* Anna smiled, still picturing Joe and Harvey. Those two sure were an apronful of laughs. *It's amazing, given their circumstances, they can still have contentment,* Anna mused.

"You look happy. Must've had a good lunch." Linda smiled knowingly.

Anna hadn't even realized she was still grinning. She dropped her purse on the counter in the back room. "Yes, it was nice."

"Did you meet Aaron someplace?"

Anna flustered. "*Ach*, no. I just had lunch with some friends. You don't know them."

Linda raised an eyebrow but said nothing, to Anna's relief. Anna's eyes roamed the shop in search of something to change the subject.

"Should we begin putting up the Christmas decorations?" Anna asked. "Seems like most everyone else has started."

"I know. Why they put them up earlier every year is beyond me. I'd prefer to wait a few more days. At least till December."

"Do you suppose decorating early could bring in more sales?" Anna wondered aloud.

"I don't know, but I'd prefer to keep our focus on the Saviour and not on sales," Linda said, carrying a bolt of fabric under her arm and walking past Anna into the main room. "God will provide for us."

Linda's comment reminded Anna of God's provision in her cousin Jacob's upcoming visit. It would be nice having her cousin and his wife around to fellowship with and to help out. Jacob had always been a lot of fun, although he was a couple years older than Anna. She'd been closer to his sister Elisabeth in the past, who, to Anna's disappointment, had jumped the fence to the *Englisch* world. Now she wondered if she'd ever see her *Englisch* cousin again. The thought dampened Anna's spirits a bit, but she was thankful her cousin had left before she joined the church. If she'd been shunned, Anna would certainly never be able to fellowship with her again – unless she renounced her fancy ways and came under the authority of the *Ordnung*.

Aaron patiently waited on Anna's porch, sipping on a mug of hot coffee her *grossmudder* had offered him. She had invited him inside, but since Anna should be returning soon, he declined. He figured he'd better spend more time with her if he only had a month to convince her they belonged together. He pulled his pocket watch out of his trousers and checked the time again.

When he heard the clip-clop of a horse's hooves coming up the road, his eyes lit up. *Anna's home.* He marched down the steps as the buggy rounded the corner and turned in to the Smuckers' lane. When his eyes caught Anna's, he raised his hand in greeting and she waved back. Soon Anna was maneuvering Brazen to the barn and Aaron unhitched the horse and led him to his stall.

Oh no. Anna sighed when she spotted Aaron on the porch. *Lord, help me to give Aaron a chance. I'm certain this is not the way a woman is supposed to feel when she comes home to the man she loves. If we're not supposed to be together, please make it abundantly clear.* She breathed the prayer silently.

She was glad when Aaron took the reins and put Brazen up in his stall, and even more surprised when she noticed the barn had been cleaned. She looked to Aaron in wonder. "Did you do this?"

Aaron shrugged. "*Jah.* I thought that we could have more time together if I did it before ya got home."

"*Denki*, Aaron." Anna blinked, still trying to register Aaron's good deed.

"Would you like to go for a walk after ya put your things in the house?" He eyed the large bag she carried with her. "Goodness, did ya take the whole house with you today?" He chuckled.

She glanced down at her bag remembering the extra food she'd taken for Joe. "*Ach*, no. Uh…let me see if *Mammi* needs help with dinner." She quickly made her way up the porch lest she be required to explain the contents of her bag.

Aaron gallantly held the door open for her.

"You may take a seat in the *schtupp* while I speak to *Mammi*," Anna advised. After Aaron headed to the living room, she greeted her *grossmudder* in the kitchen. "How was your day?"

Mammi's face brightened. "*Wunderbaar.* I see Aaron's come to see you again. Did you invite him to stay for supper yet?"

"*Nee*. He asked me to go for a walk, but I'm a little tired," Anna said. "Besides, I need to help you with dinner."

"Nonsense. Go spend time with your beau. Supper's already in the oven and I don't need any help." *Mammi* shooed her out of the kitchen.

Anna frowned, but left the kitchen anyway. Sooner or later she'd have to face Aaron. Might as well be sooner.

Aaron's face brightened when Anna walked in to the living room and he set down the magazine he'd been reading. He patted the cushion next to him on the sofa inviting Anna to sit by him.

Reluctantly, Anna sat next to him on the couch. Aaron slipped his arm around her, but she scooted a little further away from him. "Relax, Anna. I said I wouldn't try to kiss you again. I meant it." He moved his arm back to his side. "Better?"

Anna nodded, feeling the awkwardness dissipating some. "Would you like something to drink?"

"*Nee.* Your *grossmudder* gave me a cup of coffee before you got here." He sat up taller and sniffed the air. "What is that I smell?"

"*Ach, Mammi*'s making a roast for dinner. Would you like to stay?" she asked politely.

He smiled. "Only if you want me to."

What has gotten into him? His answer caught her off guard. "Uh...*jah*. Of course, I want you to."

His entire countenance illuminated at her statement. "Then I'd love to." He raised his eyebrows seeking permission before interlacing his fingers with hers.

Anna looked down at their intertwined hands and began to relax. "How was your day?" she asked, knowing he loved to talk about his dogs.

Aaron began to speak, but then seemed to think better of it. "I'd like to hear about yours first."

This definitely wasn't the Aaron she knew. *Maybe he really is trying to change.* The thought comforted Anna. "It was fine. Business seems to be picking up a little bit now that Christmas is coming."

"That's great. Have your *grossmudder*'s quilts been selling?"

He's asking about Mammi's *quilts? Unbelievable!* "No, not really. I'm praying that they'll sell soon though. We could really use the money."

Aaron reached into his pocket then put something in her hand. "I want you to have that."

Anna's eyes widened when she glanced down at the hundred dollar bill in her hand. "*Ach,* Aaron. I couldn't take this from you." She shook her head, handing back the money.

He closed her fingers around the money and held her hand in his. "I want you to have it, Anna. You said you need the money and I want to help. I sold two pups today, so I can afford it." His penetrating gaze caught her off guard.

Truly shocked, Anna said, "*Denki,* Aaron." She placed the money into her apron pocket and sent up a quick prayer of thanks.

Mammi's voice called from the kitchen. "Supper's ready!"

Aaron held out a hand. "Shall we eat?" His eyes sparkled.

Anna placed her hand in his, allowing him to help her up. "That sounds *gut,* Aaron."

All throughout the meal, Anna couldn't believe the change in Aaron. He seemed so different, as if he'd do anything she wished. He'd been polite, helpful, and even served her and Mammi's meals for them. He actually insisted on helping Anna wash dishes after the meal, which was uncharacteristic for *any*

man she'd ever heard of. She began to wonder if maybe she really had misjudged Aaron.

As Anna and Aaron sat out on the porch after the meal, he slipped his arm around her. "You don't mind, do you?"

"*Ach*, no. It *is* a little chilly out." She rubbed her arms and pulled her shawl a little tighter.

Aaron said nothing, but took off his coat and draped it over her shoulders.

"Won't you get cold without your jacket?"

"Nah, I'm fine. Especially since I'm sitting next to you." He grinned.

"*Denki*." She smiled up at Aaron, but looked away when she allowed her gaze to linger a little longer than she should. His broad frame and pleasant face were a little too easy on the eyes.

"Anna, will you join my folks and me for supper one of these nights? I know we're supposed to keep courtin' a secret, but I'd like ya to get to know my *mamm* some. *Mammi*'s welcome to come too, of course." His eyes pleaded for a positive response.

Anna tugged on her *kapp* string. "That might be nice. I'll have to ask *Mammi* and see if she'd like to go." She was almost certain her grandmother would approve. It seemed she'd taken a liking to Aaron. Anna was sure to get an earful when she went back in to the house.

"Well, I guess I better go. Morning comes pretty quick." He stood up from the wicker chair.

Anna also stood up and handed his coat back to him. "Good-bye, Aaron."

Without even attempting an embrace, Aaron waltzed to his buggy, waved goodbye, and left Anna standing on the porch.

Speechless.

SIX

A cold wind howled through the alleyway, blowing in a few leaves from the old maple trees that lined the now-vacant streets. As a passel of colorful foliage tumbled past Joe, the rustling awakened him from his contented slumber. Morning sun had just begun to illuminate the darkened sky as the last few stars faded into the dawn. He supposed, had he been home, the roosters would have begun singing in chorus. Another cluster of leaves rumbling on the pavement found their way to the corner reminding him of spring chicks huddled together to keep warm. How many times had he begged *Mamm* and *Dat* to sleep with the hatchlings in the barn?

And how many times had he gathered leaves with *Dat* and his *brieder*, only to scatter them when jumping into the pile? An enormous mountain that sometimes stood taller than Joseph. His lips turned up momentarily at the memory of *Dat* jumping into the leaves. He hadn't done it often, but on occasion *Dat* would surprise the boys by joining their play. One time he'd even hidden himself in the leaves and jumped out to scare the boys. Unfortunately, it wasn't only the boys he had startled but also the kitten in Joe's arms. He still had scars from its claw marks; even so, he didn't harbor animosity toward the creature.

Joe glanced over at Harvey next to him, lying between their wooden crates and the brick wall. His gray whiskers rubbed against his nose with each intake of breath. Joe guessed his friend slept well, other than an occasional cough. The crates served as a crude barrier against the wind but left much to be desired by way of warmth. He would need to find more blankets for them before the snow set in. It wouldn't do for Harvey to get sick. Although Harv had been out on the streets a lot longer than he had, he still worried about his old friend.

They'd met nearly two years ago when Joseph stumbled into the small town. It had been a lengthy walk from Philly, but thankfully he'd gotten a ride with a trucker part of the way. The man had said he was traveling all the way to California and for a second Joe contemplated going with him. What would it be like all the way over on the other side of the country? He'd only been to two of the fifty United States – Ohio and Pennsylvania. Yet California seemed too far away. What if he couldn't find a ride back? Twenty-seven hundred miles was a long way to walk.

Joe had in mind to visit some friends in Pennsylvania. He'd met them at different times during his *rumspringa* and it turned out they were both from the same town and knew each other. What a small world. Now, with his current circumstances the way they were, Joe was too ashamed to see his old friends. He wasn't exactly the picture of a successful Amishman. As a matter of fact, his friends were probably already married with several kinner by now. Not only was he in the *Bann*, he was destitute. Even if his friends wanted to, the *Ordnung* forbid them to extend the right hand of fellowship to a shunned man.

Amish life would never be considered an easy life. A content life for some, *jah*, but never an easy one. Joseph had been content with the Amish life until he got to know Mary. That's when his nearly-Utopian world was turned upside down. Appearances could be deceiving. But Joe wouldn't think about that right now. It was just too painful.

Linda's blue two-door sedan rolled to a stop in front of Threads of Beauty. She debated leaving the warm comfort of her vehicle to step out into the bitter cold. Reaching for her scarf and hat, she realized someone stood outside the shop. It appeared to be one of the few homeless men that sometimes wandered the streets. She regretted the thought of asking him to leave, but accommodating vagabonds just wasn't good for business. And their business hadn't been doing all that great.

As Linda approached the door, she noticed the man gazing into the shop, his face nearly touching the glass. *Why would a man be fascinated with a quilt shop?* She was about to send him on his way when she noticed him blowing into his hands and rubbing them together. How could she turn the man away?

What if he's an angel in disguise like the Bible talks about? The thought sent an added chill up her arms.

"Good morning, Ma'am. This is a nice shop you got here," the man said.

"Thank you," she said, turning the key in the deadbolt. Linda hesitated a moment. "I usually start a pot of coffee in the mornings. I could bring you cup when it's ready."

The man's face lit up as though she'd just given him a bag of gold. "That would be wonderful."

The thought of leaving the man out in the cold pricked her conscience, but would it be safe to invite him inside? *IF IT WERE ME, WOULD YOU INVITE HIM IN?* The voice almost seemed audible. Linda blew out a breath. *Okay, Lord, but I'm trusting You to keep me safe.*

"You can see the quilts better if you step inside," Linda suggested.

"Oh." The man was clearly surprised. "All right. I – I won't touch anything."

Linda disappeared into the back room to quickly set the coffee to percolate. A couple of moments later, she returned to find the man gazing upon the quilt Anna's grandmother had made. "That's pretty amazing, isn't it?"

The man turned to face her, his eyes wide. "It looks so much like the one my *gross* – uh, my grandmother used to have on her bed. Did you make it?"

Linda released a short chuckle. "Oh no, not me. Anna, the Amish girl I have working for me – her grandmother made it."

He fingered the price tag, but didn't dare touch the quilt. "Why is this not priced higher?"

It was a simple question, but Linda was intrigued that this homeless man would know the worth of a handmade Amish quilt. "We don't have too many tourists coming through this area. They tend to pass us up for the more popular towns like Intercourse and Lancaster. Or they'll wait for a mud sale or farmers' market."

"That's too bad. I'd say you could probably get twice this much." The man scratched his scraggly beard. "Well, I better go now. My friend Harv will be wondering where I went. Thanks for the coffee."

"Would you like a refill before you go?"

"All right. Thank you."

Linda soon returned with two cups. "Here's one for your friend too."

The appreciation in the man's face said more than "thank you." Linda watched as he slipped out the door and back into the frigid air outside. He'd been the first homeless person she'd ever met, but she knew he'd made a lasting impression. Perhaps it was an angel in disguise.

Joe sipped his coffee as he made his way back to the alley he and Harvey shared. *So that's where Anna works!* He should've guessed.

Her employer seemed really nice. She reminded him a little of his Aunt Martha, who'd owned her own bakery in Ohio. Oftentimes, he and his brothers would walk to town; or if *Mamm* would let them, they'd drive the pony cart. *Aentie* Martha would always greet them with a smile and a cookie of their choice. Of course, Joseph always chose a whoopie pie. The chocolate ones with peanut butter filling had always been his favorite. She hadn't always made them. In fact, Joe was the one who'd given her the idea. They quickly became bestsellers when she made her offerings available to customers. Now she couldn't seem to make enough.

Looking back, Joe would have to say it was his aunt who made a profound impact on his life. It was her words of encouragement that provoked Joseph to eventually go to junior college. Of course, she had no idea he'd gone to college. And he was certain if she knew where her words had taken him, she wouldn't have uttered them. But he was glad she did. Otherwise, he would've been even more lost than he had been after being put in the *Bann*.

Going to school had given him a sense of purpose and a drive to become something more than a farmer. Not that there was anything wrong with farming. In fact, he loved it. But unfortunately it was the only thing he knew how to do. And you can't farm without land. So when Joe became a shunned man, he realized he needed to learn a new trade.

He had been faithful in his studies, but left college to work at a full-time job when he was offered a position by a colleague.

His friend's father had been very wealthy and owned several successful businesses. Joe enjoyed the job immensely and worked hard to do his utmost. His employer valued his work ethic and quickly promoted him to a top position within the company. Before he knew it, he was working as one of the most successful executives in the corporation. He was given an expensive company car to drive, his clothes were the best money could buy, and he dined at the most prestigious restaurants.

Until one day his world came crashing down and he lost everything.

Again.

Joe's self-esteem still hadn't recovered. He supposed *that* was the real reason he was still on the streets.

SEVEN

As a stream of cool air seeped through the flap of their buggy, Anna clenched the reins tightly. She discreetly surveyed *Mammi's* grin over the brim of her black bonnet. At least one of them was excited about supper at the Gingerich home this evening. Evidently, *Mammi* had high hopes for her and Aaron. Anna, however, still doubted that she and Aaron were a good match. They were simply too different.

Although Aaron had been thoughtful at their last meeting, Anna still sensed uneasiness. This kind, giving, selfless Aaron had been refreshingly different, but seemed out of character. Not that Aaron was all that bad or anything, really. It was just little things that Anna had picked up on here and there – kicking the cat away, practically forcing her to kiss him, and she'd never forget the incident with poor Joe.

Joe.

The thought of him and Harvey brought a smile to her lips.

Mammi's words quickly dashed her amusement. "Ah, I see. You're finally gettin' excited about seeing Aaron tonight. I wondered when your nervousness would wear off. We're almost there." *Mammi* practically sang the words, patting Anna's hand.

Ugh. What Anna really felt like doing is turning around. She'd love to be at home. If she were, she imagined she'd be climbing to the attic again in search of clothing she could offer to Joe and Harvey. Wouldn't they look spiffy in *Dat's* old broadfalls. She'd meant to have them delivered by now, but it seemed every time she set out to do it, something came up.

As she maneuvered the buggy into the Gingeriches' lane, Anna held her breath. Aaron stood near the hitching post waving, his pleased countenance evident. She managed a smile although she felt it was a falsehood. This whole courtship with Aaron seemed like a farce. So why did she agree to give Aaron another month? Eternity wouldn't be enough time to convince him that they weren't right for each other – or her that they were.

"*Hiya*," Aaron said, moving to help *Mammi* down from the buggy.

Mammi patted his hand. "You are a kind young man."

Aaron smiled up at Anna, then glanced at her grandmother. "*Denki*, Lois. Welcome to our farm."

"I'll just go on up to the house and leave you two to talk," *Mammi* said, leaving Anna alone with Aaron.

Anna promptly descended the carriage before Aaron found opportunity to assist her.

"*Ach*, I coulda helped ya down. You should have waited."

"*Denki*, Aaron. But I'm perfectly capable of exiting the buggy on my own." The less she allowed him to touch her, the better.

"Well, let me at least unhitch the horse for ya. If you want, you may go into the house and say hello to my *mamm*." He grinned. "She's been anxious to see ya. We all have."

Oh boy. This is going to be a long night. "All right, I'll do that."

"I'll be inside in just a bit," Aaron said, leading her horse out to the pasture.

Aaron glowed watching his *aldi* ascend the steps of his folks' home. Hopefully, *their* home soon. She was finally here! And he hadn't even done much to convince her to visit. She agreed willingly, which took him by surprise. Perhaps she was giving him the second chance he asked for. He just needed to make sure and certain he didn't blow it.

As the door closed behind her, he imagined Anna as his wife, walking in toting the laundry from the line. He could picture her in the kitchen, preparing supper after he came in from working all day. Visions of them talking in the living room, then retiring for the evening together filled his mind. He wouldn't allow his thoughts to linger any farther. It was difficult enough to contain himself while she was around, and indulging his thoughts only brought more temptation. If he admitted it to himself, *that* was one the main reasons he wanted to marry her.

He hurried to finish up his outdoor tasks then sauntered into the house. *Mamm* had nearly prepared a feast for the five of them. Aaron washed his hands at the back sink and glanced over to see Anna examining the contents of the refrigerator. He sidled up to her and peered into the fridge as well.

"What are we looking for?" he asked.

"*Ach*, your *Mamm* asked me to find the peanut butter spread. I don't –"

"It's right here," he said, reaching around her into the door.

"Have you two found it yet?" Aaron's mother called from the table.

Anna's face heated when she noticed his arm around her waist and she abruptly stepped away.

Aaron winked at Anna, then casually answered his mother. "*Jah*, we've got it now, *Mamm*. Anna didn't see it. It was hiding in the door."

"Everything's ready now," Lois proclaimed.

"Well, if the two love birds would like to sit down, we can begin," Aaron's father said with a knowing look.

Blushing furiously, Anna took a seat next to *Mammi*. She glanced up at Aaron who winked again. She wished he would stop doing that. *Mammi* squeezed her hand and smiled before they bowed their heads in silent prayer. *Dear* Gott, *please let this night pass quickly*, Anna prayed.

After a somewhat pleasant dinner, Aaron beckoned Anna outside. Reluctantly, she followed him to the expansive veranda which wrapped around the front of the house. By the tasteful furniture in their home, although still simple, Anna suspected the Gingerich family were well-off. She suspected good-looking Aaron wouldn't have a difficult time finding a mate after they parted ways.

"Come, sit here." Aaron patted the space next to him on the oversized porch swing.

Anna lowered herself onto the swing, purposely keeping her distance.

"I'm glad you came tonight. I wasn't sure if you would."

Anna bit her lip, unsure of how to respond. She didn't wish to lead Aaron on, but neither did she desire to hurt his feelings. She wouldn't tell him that she would have rather stayed home. "*Denki* for inviting us, Aaron. I know *Mammi* had a *gut* time."

Aaron's face brightened, then suddenly dimmed a little. "About the comment my *dat* made, I hope it didn't embarrass you. I..." His voice trailed off as he seemed to gather the courage to say what was next. "I hope you'll come again." His voice was almost pleading.

"Aaron, I..." How could she say this? She stood from the swing and walked over to the porch railing. "I'm sorry, Aaron. This is just not going to work between us."

Aaron came behind her and gently grasped her upper arms. "Please, Anna, I'm trying," he whispered over her shoulder.

"You said you'd give me a chance. Unless…" He dropped his hands. "There's someone else, isn't there?"

Anna turned to face him, looking into his disappointed gaze. "*Nee*, there isn't, Aaron."

"Then why? Why am I not good enough for you?" Aaron gestured to the farm. "Look around you, Anna. All this can be yours – ours. You and *Mammi* will never have to worry about money again. We can sell your farm and –"

"You'd want to sell our home?" Anna's eyes widened. "*Mammi* grew up in that house, I would never ask her to give it up."

"But imagine the money we could get for it. In today's market –"

"See, Aaron, *this* is why it won't work between us. We don't see eye to eye." Anna sighed and started toward the front door. "*Mammi* and I should go."

"Please don't, Anna."

She turned back before entering. "I'm sorry, Aaron."

EIGHT

With Thanksgiving approaching rapidly, Anna thought again of Harvey and Joe. Had they ever enjoyed a wonderful *gut* Thanksgiving dinner with loved ones all around? Did they have family somewhere? If they did have family, were their families aware they were living on the streets?

She realized she didn't know anything about the two men, nor did they know much about her. But how familiar did she want to get with perfect strangers? Yet, they didn't seem like strangers to her; they felt more like old friends.

Anna wondered what *Mammi* would say if she knew she'd been feeding strangers – two homeless men at that. She was certain *Mammi* would worry and put an abrupt stop to her activities. But how could she just walk on by and pretend Joe and Harvey didn't exist? She could not. It seemed that her interaction with Joe and Harv had not only changed her thoughts, but her heart as well.

She wished she could invite Harvey and Joe into her home for Thanksgiving, but was certain *Mammi* would not approve.

Anna knew *Mammi* already worried about her enough. How much more anxious would she be if Anna brought home two scruffy male guests?

Anna sighed, wondering what the Lord would have her do. She'd have to pray on it for sure and for certain.

Joe had been toying with the idea for a while. Ever since he'd had that conversation with Linda, in fact. How could he help Anna out? She'd been so kind to him and Harv and he desired to pay her back somehow. If his idea worked, he'd be helping out both Anna and Linda at the same time, but he'd have to move fast. He determined to talk to Linda today to get her permission, then he'd set the wheels in motion as soon as possible.

"Oh look, it's snowing outside!" Anna smiled, remembering the fond times she and her siblings had growing up. The first snow of the season was always a welcome treat – at least it was for Anna. She'd always run outside and try to catch as many snowflakes in her mouth as possible. She was tempted to do it now, but it would have to wait for a more appropriate time. Still, the desire kindled inside her soul.

Linda stood at her side and peered out the window. "It sure is. You'd better leave early tonight."

"I'll be all right," Anna assured. "The buggy usually does just fine in the snow. And I know Brazen likes the cold weather."

"You're sure? Because I could give you a ride if it begins snowing too heavily."

"Thank you, but that won't be necessary. I've driven in the snow many times." Anna took her seat behind the counter again and picked up her knitting basket. "Do you think the snow will slow our sales?" She attempted to keep the concern out of her tone, but apparently Linda had picked up on it anyway.

"Inevitably." Linda shared an understanding glance with Anna.

"I was hoping that at least one of Mammi's quilts would sell."

"I really wish I could pay you more, Anna, but it's just not feasible," Linda said. "I'll understand if you need to find a job elsewhere that brings in more income."

Anna had considered that option in the past, but she enjoyed working with Linda. Besides, there weren't too many places that would hire a woman with only an eighth grade education. If there were, the pay wouldn't be much different than working at Threads of Beauty. Perhaps she could take on a second job. But if she did, who would tend to all the chores on the farm?

As Anna silently deliberated over these issues, she couldn't help but wonder if she'd made a mistake by dismissing Aaron's proposal. What if she and *Mammi* couldn't make ends meet and they lost the farm? Being married to Aaron and having a roof over her and *Mammi's* heads was certainly better than the alternative. Not that she and Mammi would be out on the streets like Harvey and Joe. No, the Amish took care of their own. She knew she and *Mammi* would be welcomed into the home of another Amish family, if need be. But she just couldn't wrap the thought of being married to Aaron around her mind – or her heart.

If Joe had known it was going to snow today, he wouldn't have traveled so far from 'home.' But he had to make a trip to the library to see if his idea was even possible. Linda had been very accommodating and had even agreed to keep Anna oblivious to his clandestine activities. At first Linda had seemed skeptical, but she eventually consented to his proposition. After all, she wasn't really in a position to decline something that could potentially grow her business by leaps and bounds – which is exactly what Joe had hoped would eventually happen.

Up ahead, flashing lights from a buggy stranded on the side of the road brought back unwanted memories. An image of Mary lying in the ditch flashed in his mind. *No!*

Without another thought, he rushed to the buggy. "Are you all right?" he blurted, out of breath from his mad dash to reach the buggy. He looked up and peered into familiar eyes. "Anna?"

"*Ach*, Joe. I'm so thankful it's you. I think my wheel is stuck." She moved to get down from her seat, but Joe quickly halted her.

"No. You stay there," he insisted. "I'll try to get it out. Keep hold of the reins." He quickly moved to the back wheel and noticed snow had now covered over half of it. He tried pushing first, but it wouldn't budge. He'd have to dig it out. It was times like this a shovel would come in handy.

As though reading his thoughts, Anna called to him from the front and informed him that she kept a small shovel in the box in back of the buggy. He opened the back flap and found the shovel. With the snow falling fast, Joe knew he had to work quickly or they'd both be found frozen to death by morning. Of course, he'd never allow that to happen to sweet Anna.

Anna watched out the side buggy flap while Joe continued to shovel snow. What had he been doing out on the highway? Not that she had any inkling what he usually did on a daily basis. Now she was curious, though.

"I found the culprit," Joe grinned, holding up a large rock. He threw it to the side. "And the snow didn't help either."

"Thank you, Joe. I really appreciate your help. I don't know what I would have done if you hadn't come along." She scooted over and patted the seat next to her. "Let me give you a ride back to town."

Joe nodded in appreciation and stepped into the buggy. The closed flaps blocked out most of the cold around them, but it was still chilly. Anna looked forward to standing in front of the woodstove at home. But what about Joe and Harvey? How did they stay warm – or even alive – on nights like this?

"Where were you going? If you don't mind my asking." Anna voiced her thoughts.

"Home. I…uh…had some errands to run," he said, not bothering to expound.

"Oh." Anna didn't feel like she should pry anymore. It wasn't any of her business what errands Joe was running. "I was going home."

Joe chuckled. "I kinda figured that."

"Joe, I…" Anna's voice trailed off. She wasn't sure how appropriate it would be to ask about his past.

"Did you want to say something?" He quirked an eyebrow.

"Well, you and Harvey…how did you end up on the streets?" She glanced at Joe, then focused her attention back on the road. It seemed the snow had begun falling a little faster.

"Honestly, I don't know too much about Harv. He pretty much keeps things to himself. But I know he's been through a lot."

"So you are not related to him?"

Joe laughed. "No. I met Harv about two years ago – that's when I stumbled into town. He had a problem with alcohol. I think he picked up the habit after he returned from Vietnam. He's a lot different now."

"I've never seen him drink."

"He doesn't anymore. I kind of took care of that. Anytime he'd bring home alcohol, I'd dump it out. Boy, did he get upset about that! But he was ruining his life and I couldn't watch him do that." Joe rubbed his hands together. "Harv has become a good friend to me."

Anna smiled. "I can tell."

"Sure, we tease each other and all, but I kinda feel like were kin now."

"And what about you? What's your story?"

"I'd rather not say."

"Oh, I didn't mean to pry. I just..." Anna thought a moment. "Would you mind me asking your age?"

"Twenty-five. And you?"

"Twenty-two," Anna answered, then tried to picture him without his facial hair. "I'd never guess you're only twenty-five; you look so much older. I'm sorry, that didn't come out right."

Joe laughed. "I guess this scraggly beard does make me look old."

Anna maneuvered the buggy down the street to where the alley was located. "There's Harvey. It looks like he might be worried."

"Yeah, he tends to do that."

She pulled Brazen's reins, bringing the buggy to a stop. "Thank you for helping me, Joe."

"No problem." Joe placed a caring hand over hers. "You're freezing. Come and warm up a little bit before you head home. I'm sure Harvey has a fire going."

"A fire?"

"You better believe it!" Harvey bellowed, offering Anna a hand to help her down. "How do you think we folks stay alive out here? Come, fair lady, and warm yourself by the fire for the journey home."

Anna allowed the older man to assist her, and Joe quickly moved to tether the horse. Harvey led her to a round metal trash receptacle where a small fire blazed. She briefly wondered if they'd ever been given a citation for having a fire in town. Perhaps the law enforcement officers had mercy on the destitute. What else could they have done to keep themselves warm?

Joseph soon joined Anna and Harvey and they each took a turn sharing a happy memory involving wintertime activities. Anna felt their hearts knit together each day she spent time with them; it almost felt as though Harvey and Joe had become her family.

Anna knew she shouldn't stay long because she didn't want *Mammi* to become concerned. She rubbed her hands together, enjoying the fire's warmth for a few more minutes. "I need to go now. My grandmother will worry if I am not home soon," Anna said reluctantly. It would've been nice to spend more time with Harvey and Joe and get to know them better.

"Oh no, it's snowing way too much. You'll get stuck in a blizzard," Harvey protested.

"I'll drive her home," Joe volunteered.

"But I –" Anna began to protest.

"That's an excellent idea, Joe!" Harvey's face lit up and he turned to Anna. "I wouldn't be able to sleep tonight if I didn't know you'd made it home safely. All right you two, hurry and get out of here before this weather gets worse."

NINE

Joseph had been a little nervous when first driving Anna's buggy. After all, he hadn't driven one in years. And the last time he'd ridden with a *maedel*, the outcome had been disastrous. If he was still a praying man, he'd ask *Der Herr* to keep him and Anna safe. But he'd since given up on God. Joe was certain the God he believed in as a child didn't exist.

Anna seemed surprised that Joe knew how to maneuver the rig. He hadn't admitted to being Amish, but he did tell her that he'd grown up on a farm around horses. Fortunately, she didn't pry about his past, although he knew she wanted to. Anna was clearly a curious sort and if they ever became close, he'd feel compelled to share his dreadful past with her. If he told her the truth, though, she would no longer be able to fellowship with him. For most Amish sects, a man who'd been shunned in one district would also be shunned in the others.

Joe heard a gasp escape Anna's lips as they drove into her snow-covered lane. At the end of the drive near a large white barn, an enclosed buggy stood. Joseph guessed the horse belonging to the buggy waited in a warm stable. As they neared the house, a young man – whom Joe assumed was Anna's beau – stepped out onto the porch. The moment his eyes met Joe's, he realized his assumption had been correct.

"*Ach*, what's Aaron doing here?" Anna mumbled.

"Is that your boyfriend?" Joe's eyebrows rose.

"No. Used to be," she said. "I have to warn you, Joe. He may not be very kind to you."

Joe placed his hand over hers. "Don't worry about me. I've dealt with his kind for a while now." He carefully guided the horse to the barn's entrance.

He watched Aaron out of the corner of his eye as he quickly marched to Anna's side of the buggy. "Your *grossmudder* was worried about you," Aaron said, then quickly switched to Pennsylvania Deitsh so Joe couldn't understand his words. "What is *that* man doing in your buggy?" he demanded.

Joe pretended not to comprehend as their conversation continued.

Anna responded, also in *Deitsh*. "It's none of your concern. I'll ride with whom I please. He is a kind man."

Joe squelched an appreciative smile and continued to unhitch the horse.

"He's not our kind. And he is a stranger – a tramp," Aaron's voice rose.

If Joe had correctly interpreted his tone, it sounded as though perhaps Aaron might be a little jealous. He smirked.

"You need to go home, Aaron," Anna said.

"I will *not* leave you alone with him!"

Joe now stepped to Anna's side and surveyed her eyes. "Is there a problem, Anna?"

"No," Anna said in English. "Aaron was just leaving." He didn't miss the pointed look she'd given Aaron or the exasperation in her voice.

Aaron began to speak up. "I said –"

Before he realized what was happening, Anna had stepped close and pressed her soft lips to Joseph's. Out of all the things he supposed might happen on this night, this was certainly not one of them! What was she thinking?

Disgusted, Aaron huffed and stomped off – hopefully to retrieve his horse from the barn.

Joe stared into Anna's eyes and it appeared as though she was just as shocked at her behavior as he was.

"I'm sorry, Joe. I –" She began to blush profusely and Joseph thought it quite becoming.

"No, don't apologize. I understand." Joe shrugged. "You wanted to get Aaron off your back. No big deal," he said nonchalantly, hoping he could actually believe the words he spoke.

Anna seemed to sigh in relief.

Of course she wouldn't really kiss you, he chided himself. As if he'd ever have a chance with a wonderful girl like Anna.

Joe suggested to Anna that she go inside before she caught a chill. She protested first, but agreed when she spied an elderly woman – whom Joseph suspected to be her grandmother – peek out the door. He assured her that he would take care of Brazen and bring the buggy into the barn.

Aaron led his mare out of the barn and briskly hitched her up. From his buggy, his voice rang loud and clear, "If I were you, I'd watch my step around here. Don't think you stand a chance with Anna. We Amish marry our own kind." Aaron looked Joseph over in disgust. "And *you* definitely are not Anna's kind, nor will you ever be."

Who does this guy think he is? Joe certainly couldn't picture kind Anna marrying a jerk like Aaron. He was tempted to put this windbag in his place, but wouldn't out of respect for Anna. He knew she wouldn't approve.

Joe ignored his insults and moved to tend Anna's horse. Fortunately, he heard the clip-clop of Aaron's horse travel down the lane and onto the road.

Anna stared up at the ceiling although her room was nearly pitch black. She couldn't sleep. *What was I thinking?* She couldn't get over the reality of what she'd done. It had almost seemed surreal.

Did I really kiss Joe? Then she remembered the bewildered look on Joe's face – and the appalled one on Aaron's. *Of course, I did.*

Why had she done it? That's what she couldn't fathom. She'd since played the scene in her mind many times and still couldn't come up with a satisfactory reason. Except maybe that Joe was so kind and caring…or selfless…or because he had nice eyes?

Oh no, this can't be happening! Joe and I could never work, she reasoned. *I am Amish and Joe is…well…homeless. And Englisch.* But despite all the chaos of the evening and Anna's confusing thoughts, she realized one thing. Somehow, kissing Joe felt…*right.*

TEN

Joe shivered as he stumbled back into town. Not even his all-consuming thoughts of Anna's kiss could warm his chilled body. The walk had taken him much longer than it would have under pleasant weather conditions. Snow had begun falling fast and hard about halfway to his destination, making for a perilous journey. If he hadn't been moving, he'd certainly be buried under a foot or two of snow by now.

Thankfully, Anna was most likely tucked into a warm bed, safe from the extreme elements. He wouldn't want her out in this. How is it that he'd come to care so much for Anna?

He sighed when he finally rounded the corner to the alleyway. Just as he suspected, snow had built up around his and Harvey's sleeping quarters. He glanced around, but there was no sign of Harvey. Had he gone somewhere to find shelter from the snow? It wouldn't have been the first time.

"Harv, are ya here?" Joe called out.

No response.

"Harv?" Joe walked near the trash receptacle, then to the wooden crates that they typically used to shield themselves from inclement weather. The crates were completely covered, but he could still identify their form. He picked one up and brushed the snow off, surveying the area again for any trace of Harvey.

Although exhausted, he knew he wouldn't be able to sleep if he couldn't find his friend. After checking every place in the alley where he thought Harvey might be, he set off to search on foot. Downtown was quiet, but dimly illuminated by street lights. It reminded him of a painting he'd seen hanging in the dry goods store when he was a child. Fortunately, the snowfall had lessened significantly allowing Joseph to see clearly. He went to each shop in town, surveying the exterior and peeking through the windows to the interior, in hopes of finding his missing friend.

What seemed like hours later, Joe returned to the alley, took the two wooden crates, and set off for Threads of Beauty. Once there, he nearly collapsed from fatigue. The small nook at the store's entrance was probably the best place he could be. At least he'd stay partially out of the elements, and it was most likely the only place where he wouldn't be run off. Besides, he hoped that perhaps Anna and Linda would help search if Harvey hadn't returned by morning.

Aaron laid awake the entire night. He could not get the remembrance of Anna kissing that homeless guy out of his head. To think Anna would prefer a dirty, destitute beggar over him was beyond comprehension. What an insult!

What would his father say if he knew Anna had chosen a homeless man over him? No doubt he'd again be reminded that he was a failure – a loser. No, his father never said those words aloud, but it was exactly how Aaron felt when his *daed* exhibited his disappointment.

He was determined not to let that happen. He had to come up with a plan to get Anna back, but what could he do? He was unsure at the moment, but in time he would come up with some type of strategy. He had to.

Linda frowned when she pulled up to the curb. Apparently, Joe had found shelter in the alcove of her storefront. She wished there were a place these homeless men could go to find shelter, but the nearest place she knew of was many miles away. She couldn't blame them for preferring the small-town atmosphere over a larger city. But Linda wondered how they survived. Did they live solely on the good graces of others?

She thought for a moment about Joe's proposition a few days before. If his idea worked, she wouldn't mind paying him some. It would be great to be able to help someone get back on their feet again. She just hoped she wasn't making a mistake in allowing him to try out his idea. Only time would tell, she supposed.

"Joe?" she said cautiously as she neared the store's entrance. She watched as the wooden crates moved and then winced when one tumbled to the ground.

"What is it?" Joseph shot up. Apparently, she'd startled him.

"Joe, it's me. Linda."

Joe rubbed his eyes, then squinted. "Oh, sorry, Linda. I didn't sleep too well. I couldn't find Harv last night." He picked up the crates and moved them out of her way. "Have you seen him?"

"No, I haven't. Do you think he might have taken shelter somewhere?"

Joe glanced up and down the street as though hoping to spot his friend. "That's what I was thinkin'. But he usually leaves a note to let me know. I don't know where he could be. I'm kinda worried about him, ya know?"

"When did you see him last?"

"Last night before I took Anna home," he said.

Linda's eyes widened. "You took *Anna* home? Anna Smucker that works here – the Amish girl?" She was unaware Joe and Anna knew each other.

Joe nodded. "I found her stuck in the snow on the side of the road. I helped her get the buggy unstuck, then we came back here to warm up by the fire. I didn't want her driving home alone in that blizzard, so I went with her. That was when I last saw Harv. He stayed back."

"Should we call the police?"

"Oh no, Harvey wouldn't like that. Now that the sun's coming up, I hope I'll have a better chance locating him." He rubbed his bearded chin as though pondering. "Would you help me look for him? I think we might have a better chance finding him if there were two of us looking."

Linda was already chilled just being out of her car for a few moments. She certainly didn't want to go traipsing around town in this weather. But she didn't have it in her heart to say no to Joe. "I'll tell you what. Let me put some coffee on for us, then we can go out searching for your friend."

Joe agreed. "That sounds good. I could use something warm. I'll take these crates back while you're making coffee, it'll help me get the blood flowing. Who knows? Maybe Harv's back already."

Linda watched as Joe picked up the crates and made his way down the street. She sent up a silent prayer that they'd be able to find Harvey and that he'd be okay.

Where could she be? Anna peeked through the window of Threads of Beauty. It appeared the lights were on, but the doors were locked and Linda was nowhere in sight. Linda had always opened thirty minutes before Anna arrived to turn the heater on and start a pot of coffee. She usually had coffee and cookies on hand throughout the day for the customers to enjoy while they browsed. Perhaps she'd gone out to the store to purchase more cookies?

Anna glanced down the street toward the alley where Joe and Harvey lived. She hated the fact that they had to be out in the snow all hours of the night. If only she could do something for them. Maybe they could live in the barn? At least during the freezing temperatures in winter. It wouldn't be much, but at least then they'd be out of the harsh weather. She knew *Mammi* would never approve if she brought them home. But what if *Mammi* didn't know?

And Aaron. He'd no doubt have a conniption if Joe and Harv moved into the barn. A wry smile formed on Anna's lips. She was almost determined to bring them home for that reason alone. But of course Aaron would report her to the bishop for sure and for certain.

Anna sent up a silent prayer for wisdom. She didn't know what she could do, but she knew what she *couldn't* do. She couldn't sleep peacefully every night knowing that Joe and Harvey were outside sleeping in an alley with no shelter at all while she was tucked into a warm bed.

"Is this where you last saw him?" Linda glanced around the quiet, snow-covered alley.

"Yep. We usually sleep over there near the corner. With the crates and the garbage can, it seems to be the best place to stay.

Of course, it doesn't keep us completely out of the elements but it helps. The high walls keep a lot of the wind out," Joseph said.

Linda walked over to the large trash receptacle and peered inside. There was no sign of Harvey, but the foul odor nearly caused her to wretch. *How could anyone live this way?*

"There aren't many places Harv could be here. I already checked that dumpster."

"No, he doesn't appear to be here." Linda listened carefully. Had she heard something? Perhaps a cat?

Meow.

Linda looked around but saw nothing. "Where is that coming from?"

"Mama Kitty. That's what we call her, although we've never actually seen her kittens. Just the evidence that she must've had a litter." Joseph smiled. "She comes around every once in a while asking for food." He peeked into the receptacle after hearing the faint sound of banging metal. "Not here." He slowly walked around the dumpster. "Ah, I see."

Linda watched as a pathetic calico cat emerged from a small tunnel under the garbage container.

Joe picked up the famished feline and brushed the snow off her back. "Seems like someone's found a shelter from the snow." The cat licked his hand. "Sorry, girl. I don't have anything for you right now."

Linda smiled at the gentle way he handled the animal, but quickly turned again to the dumpster. "That noise again."

"Harv?" Joseph set the cat down and crouched near the small tunnel. "Are you in there?" He furiously began digging with his bare hands when they heard a moan. "Just wait, Harv. I'll get you out."

"Oh no, he must be freezing under there." This didn't look good. "Should I call an ambulance?" She looked on as Joseph pulled Harvey out from under the dumpster. He laid his friend across his lap and placed a hand on his neck to feel for a pulse.

Harvey's eyes popped open. "No ambulance."

Joe released a sigh of relief. "Harvey, you're alive!"

"Of course, I'm alive." The older man struggled to his feet. "You ain't getting' rid of me that easy." He began coughing profusely.

Linda spoke up. "We need to get him warm. I have some blankets in my back room and one in the trunk of my car if we need it. Harvey, do you think you can walk to my shop?"

"I'll help him," Joe offered, placing an arm around the older man's back.

Harvey glanced over at Linda and grinned. "Looks like we got us another angel, Joe."

Anna's eyes widened at the peculiar sight of Joe, Harvey, and Linda coming up the sidewalk. *What's Linda doing with Joe and Harv?* As they came closer, she realized something wasn't right.

Linda moved ahead and quickly placed her key in the lock. "I'm sorry for not being here, Anna. Joe needed my help."

Her gazed moved toward Joe's face and she recalled their nearness from the night before.

He smiled slightly, obviously troubled over something. "I couldn't find Harv last night, but fortunately, Linda and I found him this morning."

Her examining gaze swept over Harvey, who appeared sallow. "Well, hello there, Miss An –" his words were abruptly cut off by a fit of coughing.

Anna didn't miss the worry that creased Joe's brow. His compassion for others gripped her heart once again. What was this young man's story and how is it that one so concerned for others not have anyone to care for him? Or did he? Is it possible that Joe did indeed have a family somewhere?

They moved into the store and were immediately enveloped in warmth. Anna watched as Linda led Joe and Harvey to the back room, wondering what had transpired between the time Joe left her home last night and this morning. Since there were no customers yet, she followed after them.

"Here, sit him down in this chair," Linda suggested, handing Harvey a mug of steaming coffee once he was seated. "Anna, bring that small heater I keep in the cabinet."

Anna hastily did as Linda suggested while Joe removed Harvey's wet shoes and socks and Linda draped blankets around Harv. She positioned the small heater to warm Harv's feet.

"How's that feel, buddy?" Joseph asked his friend, rubbing his arms to produce warmth.

Anna remembered a trick she'd once learned while working as a *maut* for some *Englisch* neighbors as a teen. She took a hand towel from one of the drawers and put it in the microwave for several seconds to warm it. She checked to be sure it wasn't too hot, then brought it to Harvey and placed it over his face. "Does that feel nice?" she asked.

"Y'all make me feel like I'm at some fancy hotel spa," Harvey said.

"Ah, quit makin' a fuss, Harv." Joe smiled catching Anna's eye.

Anna returned his grin. It was good to see some of Joe's anxiety relieved. The sound of a bell jingling reminded Anna that she had a job to do. "I better go wait on our customer." With that, she slipped into the store's main floor room.

ELEVEN

*A*nna glanced at Joe and Harvey in the back seat of the buggy and pretended not to be as nervous as she felt. *How am I going to explain this to Mammi?* Of course, it wasn't as though she had a choice. She wasn't about to leave them out in the snow, especially with Harv in his fragile condition.

Although Joe had cared for Harvey in the store's backroom most of the day, he still had a ways to go before being out of the woods. It seemed Harvey had developed a horrid cough akin to croup. Anna knew *Mammi* must have an herbal cure for his ailment, but she was quite certain proper nourishment, plenty of fluids, and adequate rest would probably do the trick. At least that's what Anna had realized with past experience. Part of healing was simply allowing the sickness to run its course and providing the necessary nutrition for the body to do what God intended.

"I apologize that you'll have to stay up in the haymow," Anna voiced her thoughts.

"Oh no, Anna, don't you feel bad." Joe gently touched her arm, communicating his gratitude. "This will be better than any place we've stayed in a long time. Just to be out of the snow will be a blessing."

"I have a small heater you can use, but I'll have to bring out the extra blankets after *Mammi* has gone to bed. There are a couple of buggy blankets you can use until I come."

Harvey spoke up. "I was right, Joe. Your Anna is an angel."

"You just might be right about that, Harv," Joe said.

Anna sighed with contentment. It felt good to help others out. She didn't have much extra, but what she did have she was happy to share with her new friends. And why not? Isn't that why God had given her material blessings – so she could in turn bless others? It was as though God's hand were reaching down to Anna and she reached her hands to Harvey and Joe, creating a circle of love.

Anna's gaze caught Joe's and he offered a genuine smile.

Love? Yes, that's exactly what it was.

"Oh good, you're finally here!" *Mammi's* smile illuminated the room. "I have some wonderful news. Jacob and Rachel will be here a week early."

"You mean…in two days?" Anna gulped.

"If not sooner. Isn't it wonderful *gut* news?" *Mammi* moved to the already-set table with a large pot of corn chowder. "Come, sit down so we can eat." She placed a loaf of bread next to the soup.

Anna sat down, but she thought she might be too nervous to eat. She noticed a bouquet of flowers in the middle of the table. "The flowers look nice, *Mammi.*"

"Don't they? Well, I was waiting to tell you but I guess I might as well come out with it."

Anna raised her eyebrows.

"Your beau brought those by today. Isn't that nice? That Aaron seems like such a *gut* young man." *Mammi* grinned. "He also did some work in the barn."

Anna's face reddened. Was this some ploy to get her back? "I'm not seeing Aaron anymore."

"I know that, dear. But can't you give him a chance?" *Mammi* ducked her head and spoke quietly, "I...uh...invited him to join us for Thanksgiving."

"What? *Mammi*, why would you do that? I already told you —"

Mammi placed her hand on top of Anna's. "I'm sorry. It's just that...he asked and I couldn't turn him down."

He asked? Anna scooted her chair back and abruptly rose from her seat. Heat rose to her cheeks and coursed through her veins. *The nerve of him!* She grabbed the vase from the table and tossed the flowers into the trash can. With hot tears streaming down her cheeks, she stormed up the stairs to her room. She didn't know if she was more upset with Aaron for forcing himself into her life or *Mammi* for doing his bidding.

Joe quickly turned the flashlight off when he heard the barn door squeak open, just in case it wasn't Anna entering. He hid from sight and hoped Harv wouldn't erupt into another coughing fit. Perhaps staying in Anna's barn wasn't such a great idea after all. The last thing he desired was to get sweet Anna into trouble with her bishop. He knew all too well the possible outcome in such a circumstance. Anna had been so kind to offer the barn as a refuge while Harvey healed from his ailment and he wouldn't think of causing her undue stress in return for her graciousness.

"Joe?" Anna's quiet voice echoed up the ladder.

Joe turned the flashlight back on. "We're still here, Anna."

"Oh, good, you're awake. I didn't want to wake Harv up if he was resting." Her head appeared at the top of the ladder and she handed Joseph a thermos. "Here, I brought some soup for you and Harvey. I'm sorry it's so late. It seemed *Mammi* stayed up extra-long tonight."

"It's fine."

"I forgot to mention that we have an old outhouse just outside the back of the barn." She removed a backpack from her shoulders and pulled some clothing out. "And here. These are some of my father's clothes. I think they might be a little large for you, but his suspenders are in there too."

"Won't your father need them?" he asked in concern.

"*Ach*, no. My father died last year." She bowed her head.

"I'm sorry, Anna." Joe placed his hand over hers. "Thank you for this kindness."

"He would want them to be put to good use." Anna smiled. "Besides, I'd like to see you and Harv in Amish clothes."

Joe's eyebrows raised. "Do you think we'll make good Amishmen?"

"Well, I don't know. We'll just have to wait and see how *gut* you can work," she teased.

Joseph laughed. "Ah, I knew there was a catch!"

Harvey spoke up now. "Would you two stop flirting and get me some of that soup. This poor man's dying over here and you two act like you're out courtin' under a full moon."

Joe caught the beautiful pink stain that tinged Anna's ivory cheeks. "Yes, sir." He winked at Anna.

"I better go now," Anna said. "Just in case *Mammi* realizes I'm not there."

"Thank you, Anna," Joe reiterated.

"Is there anything else you need?" Anna's hand flew to her forehead. "Oh no, I forgot the blankets."

"That's all right. These should be fine, especially with the heater," Joe assured. He heard Harvey clearing his throat, reminding him of his desire for soup. "I'm coming, I'm coming, Harv. You're such a big baby when you're sick."

"Well, someone's gotta take care of this old man."

"I'll say goodnight now," Anna said.

Joe watched Anna's lovely face disappear and heard evidence of her exit when the barn door squeaked again.

"You oughta marry that girl, Joe," Harv commented.

Joe didn't admit it to Harv, but he was thinking the exact same thing. The problem was – well, actually, there were many problems. Of course, nothing couldn't be overcome through sheer determination and will power. He'd learned that in the past. But if he even stood a chance with Anna, he'd have to become Amish again. And that meant repenting in his district before Bishop Burkholder – something he was not willing to do. Ever.

When Anna awoke this morning, she never expected what now lay before her eyes. As she hit the bottom step, she nearly tripped over her own two feet. *What are Joe and Harvey doing at the breakfast table? Oh no,* Mammi *is not going to like this!* She must get them outside quickly before *Mammi* came out of her room.

Mammi walked into the room, a pair of scissors in her hand. *Too late.*

Anna cringed waiting for *Mammi's* reaction.

"Look who I found out in the barn this morning, Anna. Your friends, Joe and Harv." *Mammi* gave Anna a pointed look.

Anna looked on helplessly. "I…I can explain. You see –"

"No need. Harvey has already explained everything. We can talk about this later." *Mammi* set the scissors on the counter and handed Harvey a cup of hot herbal tea. "All right, Joe.

You're first." She beckoned him to the chair in the middle of the kitchen.

"What are you doing?" Anna asked, still bewildered at the scene before her.

Joe shrugged. "Your grandmother said if we're going to be under her roof we gotta be clean and look nice." He grinned. "We already had a bath."

"And that means a haircut too," *Mammi* insisted. "I don't know how you can even see with all that hair. A man should keep his hair short. And after this, I want you to go and cut off all that face hair. Only married and old men should have beards. There's an old razor you can use too. It's in the cabinet."

"Yes, Ma'am."

Anna wanted to burst into laughter. She could only imagine what had taken place prior to her rising. Harvey quickly filled her in while *Mammi* cut Joe's hair.

Apparently, *Mammi* had stepped outside in the early morning to retrieve a few items she'd forgotten on the clothesline and inadvertently heard Harv's coughing. *Mammi* already suspected something was up when she'd heard Anna going out the night before. Joe had been in the outhouse when *Mammi* entered the barn.

"Who's up there?" Mammi *demanded.*

Harvey's bright face peeked over a hay bale. "Well, now. If I haven't seen a more beautiful being in all my life."

Mammi*'s face turned five shades of pink, Harv had said. "Who are you and what are you doing in my barn?"*

"I guess that's a fair question. But if I tell you my name, you're going to have to tell me yours, pretty lady." He patiently waited for her response.

"I will do no such thing."

"All right, pretty lady. Then I guess I'll just have to tell ya how I got to be here. A sweet angel named Miss Anna brought me and my friend Joe here. I've been sick, ya see, and Anna and Joe are helping me to get better."

"Anna is my granddaughter."

"Oh no, you look much too young to be Anna's grandmother. I see the years have been very kind to you," Harvey charmed.

Mammi *stammered, "Th-the barn is no place for a sick person."*

At that point, Joe had entered the barn. *"We're really sorry if we're intruding, Ma'am. But I didn't want to leave Harv out in the snow in his condition, so when Anna offered the barn, we gladly accepted. But we can leave if you don't want us here."*

Mammi *seemed to take in their present condition, eyeing their tattered clothing. "Are you telling me the two of you have no home?"*

"Yes, Ma'am."

At that point, compassion seemed to replace contempt. *"Well, then I suppose Anna did the right thing. You must come in and have some breakfast."*

Anna smiled, picturing the whole scene. She almost wished she could've been a fly on the wall.

TWELVE

*A*nna embraced *Mammi* and whispered a silent 'thank you' before retrieving her coat. *Mammi* had offered the small *dawdi haus* to Joe and Harvey, but insisted they earned their keep. Both men happily agreed to the arrangement. With all the excitement this morning, Anna was now running late.

Joe emerged from the restroom just in time to stop her. "May I catch a ride into town with you?"

The sight of Joe made Anna feel as though a music box dancer performed inside her heart. She didn't expect Joe to look so young...or handsome. Not that he wasn't handsome before. But now that she could actually see his face – what a difference a haircut and the absence of facial hair made. Of course, seeing him in Amish clothes persuaded her judgment a little too. *He's not Amish,* she reminded herself.

"Anna?" he asked again.

Anna peeled her eyes off him. "Oh, uh, I'm sorry." She hoped her countenance didn't manifest her thoughts. Anna turned to her grandmother. "*Mammi,* do you mind if Harv stays here with you?"

"I'll see to it that Harvey gets his herbs and lunch. He's already resting now, so hopefully he won't get underfoot today," *Mammi* said. "You go on ahead. Joe already cleaned the barn this morning and brought the eggs in, so he's free until this evening."

"I appreciate that, Ma'am," Joseph said with a chuckle.

"Thanks, *Mammi.*" Anna followed Joe out the door. He quickly moved to hitch up the horse to the buggy and Anna thought it odd that he knew precisely how everything connected. But then she remembered he'd told her that he once had Amish neighbors.

"All set." He smiled. "Shall I drive or would you like to?"

"You may." Anna thought it was nice to have a man beside her as she traveled; somehow, Joe made her feel safe. As they rode along, she wondered why Joe had wanted to come.

"It looks like it's going to be a nice day. The sun feels good, doesn't it?" He briefly closed his eyes to breathe in the fresh scents, obviously enjoying the ride.

"What are your plans for the day?"

Joe scratched his head. "Well, I plan to go to the library."

Anna laughed. "Really?"

"Why do you laugh?"

Anna sensed a bit of offense. "Oh no, I didn't mean…I guess you just don't seem like the library type to me."

He raised his eyebrows. "The library *type*? I don't think I get you."

"You know, nerdy and super smart...not that you're dumb or anything. Oh boy, it seems nothing I say is coming out the right way. I'll just close my mouth now. Forget about what I said."

"So, are *you* the library type?"

"No comment. I said to forget the former conversation, remember?"

"Only if you'll have lunch with me." He smiled. "*Mammi* packed us plenty."

"Deal. Where?"

"That depends on how long you've got today."

"An hour."

"Well then it'll be a surprise."

"But I –"

"Don't you like surprises?" He grinned.

"Yes, but –"

"It's a surprise," Joe stated firmly. Before she could answer again, he brought his fingers to her lips to silence her. "This is where you simply nod your head in compliance," he teased.

Anna opened her mouth to protest, then thought better of it and closed her mouth again. She finally spoke up. "I can't believe you told me to shut up."

"Well, I hoped to sound a little more polite."

"Of course, Joe. Everything you say is polite. I can't picture you not speaking politely."

"You didn't hear me with Aaron the other day after you kissed me."

"Oh no, don't mention Aaron. Or the kiss." She winced.

"Why not? I liked the kiss."

Anna's cheeks heated. "You did?"

"In a disturbed, shocked, and slightly surprised kinda way." He smiled.

"What did you say to Aaron?"

"Nothing. I was just teasing you."

Anna shook her head. "That's just like you, Joe – taking the high road. I admire you."

Joseph's face brightened. "You do?"

Anna nodded.

Joe placed his hand on Anna's. "Thank you, Anna. No one's ever said anything like that to me before."

Their eyes locked briefly, then Joseph removed his hand. Anna looked out at the *Englischers* in their cars. She figured they must look like a young courting couple to passersby, or perhaps even a young married couple.

She glanced back at Joe and frowned. They'd never have a chance at love, which she was certain was what this was, because she was Amish and he was not. Tears pricked her eyes, but she quickly brushed them away. It wasn't good for either of them to be spending this much time together. If they continued, Anna was certain she'd lose her heart for good.

"Well, here we are," Joe said, pulling up to Threads of Beauty. "I'll be here at twelve then?" His eyes sparkled and Anna still couldn't get over how handsome he was.

"Uh, no. Joe, I think it's better if we don't have lunch together." Anna hopped down from the buggy, then reached for the lunch container. She quickly opened it to retrieve her sandwich, doing her best not to meet Joe's eyes.

Joe set the brake on the buggy, then reached for Anna's hand and clasped it tight. "Why, Anna?"

She couldn't help the tears that pricked her eyes once again. "You know why. It can never work between us."

"Yes, it can. You know we're perfect for each other, Anna. Love can conquer anything." His eyebrows lowered and Anna caught the desire in his eyes. Not a lustful desire, but a desire to make their relationship work, a desire to fight for her love. She heard his unspoken plea loud and clear.

But he'd never understand. How could he? In some ways, it seemed things were simpler in the *Englisch* world. You could marry whomever you chose, as long as you promised to love your spouse. There were no extra rules you had to follow. You didn't have to sacrifice romantic love for familial love and acceptance. You were free.

But Anna wasn't free. Being with Joe meant she would have to leave *Mammi* all alone, and she could never do that. Anna had never doubted her faith before, but now it seemed so constricting. Here was Joe, quite possibly the sweetest man she'd ever met, offering his love to her. How could she reject it?

But she had to…there was no other way.

"I'm so sorry, Joe," Anna's voice faltered. She rushed from the buggy and into the store as quickly as she could.

Linda's gaze lifted from her sewing project to Anna's hasty entrance. She immediately noticed tears streaming down her cheeks. "Anna, what's wrong?"

Anna shook her head. "Will you let Joe know that you're taking me home today?"

"I am?"

"Could you, please?"

"Well, yes." Linda nodded. "Okay, I'll tell him."

Linda quickly made it out the door as Joe was pulling away. "Joe!" She hoped he'd heard over the sound of the horse's hoof beats.

The buggy's abrupt stop indicated he had. Linda rushed to the carriage. "Anna said to tell you she doesn't need a ride home today. You may go back anytime you'd like."

Joe nodded solemnly and Linda noticed his clean, youthful appearance. "You look nice, Joe. How's Harvey doing?"

His face brightened a little at the mention of Harv. "A lot better. Thank you for allowing him to recuperate in your store."

"It was no problem." Linda remembered their private conversation the other day. "About our plans…are they still on?"

Joe nodded. "Still on. I'm going back to the library today. Hopefully, that will set the wheels in motion. You haven't said anything to Anna yet, have you?"

"No."

"Good. I don't want her to know."

Linda noticed Joe's eyes misting. *What is wrong with these two?* She wanted to find out, but she wouldn't ask Joe. Perhaps she could get something out of Anna. "I'll let you go now."

Joe's buggy disappeared into the light traffic and Linda hurried back into the shop.

THIRTEEN

Concentration proved difficult for Joseph, as he sat at a desk in the library. The computer screen in front of him blurred as he gathered his emotions. His heart hadn't been in this much turmoil since Mary's death, and of course, his excommunication.

Why had he opened up his heart to Anna? It seemed like anytime he invested himself in someone, heartache eventually followed. First, it had been Mary. Then he'd lost his family and his community. Next, his co-workers turned their backs on him believing lies instead of the truth. And now Anna.

This is why he'd turned his back on God. No matter how kind Joe was, no matter how much he poured his time, talents, and love into people, he still ended up losing. But he couldn't live any other way. He'd tried being mean and selfish, but it only made him feel miserable inside. He had to be true to himself.

And of course, that was why he was here at the library. He promised Linda he would try to help and he would keep that promise. No matter if what he was doing didn't produce any fruit. No matter if it produced a lot of fruit and he didn't receive any reward. People were counting on him.

Joe swiped his eyes, gathered his resolve, and began typing away at the keyboard.

Anna felt miserable as she, *Mammi*, and Harv sat at the supper table. Joe had chosen to stay in the *dawdi haus*. She hadn't seen him since he dropped her off at work this morning. Anna wondered where he'd gone after he left. *Mammi* said he hadn't returned home until late afternoon, so he must've gone somewhere besides the library.

She was glad to see that Harvey was regaining his strength. No telling what kind of bitter herbal teas *Mammi* had made him drink throughout the day. She'd drank many throughout the years. They were difficult going down sometimes, but they always worked.

Tomorrow Jacob and Rachel were scheduled to arrive and Anna was looking forward to it. There was nothing like family and the little ones, especially, to lighten the heart. It seemed like lately hardship was all they knew, but Anna realized she still had plenty to be thankful for. God was always faithful. Always.

Harv entered the *dawdi haus* and closed the door behind him. "When are you going to talk to her?"

"I'm not," Joe said.

"You have to, Joe."

"No, I don't."

"Well, then you're a fool. That woman loves you," Harvey stated.

Joe grimaced. "Stay out of this, Harv. It doesn't concern you."

"You're saying that I shouldn't be concerned about two of the best people I know. Two people that are miserable because neither one of them will speak to the other." Tears formed in Harvey's eyes. "Don't let her slip out of your hands, Joe. It's not worth it." Harv swiped at his eyes. "I never told you this before, but I was once married."

Joseph sat up and stared at Harvey. "You were?"

"Yep. Virginia. She was a perty little thing."

"What happened?"

Harv explained, "It was 1967 when Virginia and I met. She was a waitress at a little coffee shop I frequented while in college. We spent a lot of time just getting to know each other and became good friends. After several months passed, we began dating and I took her home to meet my folks - that's what we did back in those days, you know. Anyway, by the end of the year Virginia and I were married. By spring, we had a little one on the way. Boy, were we excited!

"Got a letter in the mail from the President of the United States. Apparently, they needed a few good men to go off to Viet Nam and so I was drafted. My little one was born and buried while I was over there. I never got to see him or hold him in my arms. But Virginia said he was beautiful, she said he looked like me. I reckon I was handsome back then.

"When I finished my tour of duty and service to my country, I'd heard the American people were not happy. I'd heard that all that awaited a soldier's return was disgrace and humiliation. So instead of bringing shame upon my beautiful Virginia, I didn't tell her that I'd returned home.

"A couple of years later, I learned that she had cancer. I couldn't help it; she needed me, and so I went to her. Boy, was she shocked to learn that I was still alive. I only got a few weeks with her before she passed. I *could* have had years. You see, Joe. She was never ashamed of me. She was here waiting for me with open arms. But I was a fool. I didn't believe our love was strong enough to withstand the trials of life, but I was wrong.

"So, don't tell me that I have no right being concerned about you and Anna. You have a love that's pure. Don't make the same mistake I made. Don't give up because of fear. And don't ever give up on God." Harvey wiped away his tears with shaky hands.

Joe shook his head. "It's too late, Harvey. I gave up on God a long time ago. He has forsaken me."

Harvey stood up, crossed his arms over his chest, and stared Joe in the face. "That is a lie straight from the devil! God promised to never leave or forsake His own. Others may have forsaken you, Joe, but God never has and He never will."

"Well, then tell me where He's been all my life. I want to know. Because He sure hasn't offered His hand to help me out," Joe spat out bitterly.

"Open your eyes and look around you, Joe. If this isn't God's providence, then I don't know what is."

Joseph opened his mouth to protest, but he couldn't form the words. He realized Harvey was right. For the first time in years, Joe bowed his head and gave a brief prayer of thanks for God's provision.

FOURTEEN

*J*oe hadn't found an opportune time to speak with Anna yet, but perhaps it was better to wait a while. Their company was scheduled to arrive today and *Mammi* had put him to work fixing odds and ends around the house. He wasn't even sure of what he would say to Anna when he had the opportunity, but hoped the words would come. He continually wrestled with the idea of telling Anna the truth about his past, but the thing that he feared most was Anna's rejection. He couldn't decide if it was better that she continued to believe he was *Englisch*, or reveal that he'd been excommunicated from the Amish. Either way, he'd lose. There was no possible solution.

He opened the back screen door of the house to a loud squeak. It would need to be fixed. He knew the main back door also needed attention. A minute later he returned from the barn with lubricant in his hand and quickly sprayed some on the screen door's hinges. He opened the back door, which, to his surprise did not squeak, but he decided to spray it anyway. Joe stepped inside to shield himself from the cold.

"When did this come?" Joe heard Anna's distraught voice.

"Just today," *Mammi* said.

"But we don't have an extra twelve hundred dollars! They can't expect us to pay this by next month," Anna cried. "Oh *Mammi*, we're going to lose the house."

Joe knew he shouldn't be listening in on their conversation so he quickly stepped back outside. But he'd heard enough. Anna and *Mammi* were in trouble. Hopefully, God willing, he'd be able to provide the solution.

"Joe?" *Mammi* called. "Will you come in here and help me with this thing?"

"Yes, Ma'am." Joe set his glass of water on the counter, then followed *Mammi* into one of the other rooms. When he stepped into the room, he immediately noticed several folded quilts tucked into clear plastic bags that sat on top of a bureau.

"Will you help me move this quilting frame into the other room? This room's bigger than the other and I'd like to let Jacob's family use it," *Mammi* said.

"Sure," Joe said, then pointed to the quilts. "What are those for?"

"I'd planned to sell them."

"I saw the Christmas quilt that you made in Threads of Beauty. It was remarkable. One of the nicest I've ever seen."

Mammi reached over with her weathered hand and patted Joe's hand. "*Denki*, child. It is kind of you to say so. *Der Herr* had blessed me with a wonderful *grossmudder* that taught me how to quilt when I was just a *maed.*"

"She taught you well," Joe said, then picked up his end of the quilting frame.

Mammi picked up her side, then quickly set it down. "*Ach*, I better call Anna in to help with this. I don't know if I should take my chances on this old back."

Joe watched as *Mammi* disappeared and Anna returned in her stead.

"*Mammi*'s in the kitchen," Anna explained.

Joe again noticed a hint of pink in her cheeks. "We should talk."

"I'd rather not. I don't know what good it will do."

Joseph frowned. "Would you rather that Harv and I leave?"

"No. Of course not."

Voices and the pitter patter of little footsteps turned their attention to the kitchen. Anna poked her head out of the room, then quickly returned to lift her side of the quilting frame. "Looks like they're here. We'd better hurry."

"Yeah. I should go check on Harv too." Joe led the way out of the room and Anna directed him to where the quilting frame should go. After they finished, he abruptly stepped outside and headed for the *dawdi haus*. He didn't want to interrupt family time as *Mammi*, Anna, and her cousins greeted one another.

As Joseph and Harvey sat at their small table playing cards, Joe noted a knock at the door. He waited for Harv to answer the call, but his friend refused.

"I ain't got no callers. That'll be for you," Harvey insisted. "My guess is that pretty little lady."

Another knock prompted Joe to answer. Anna stood on the doorstep.

"What did I tell ya?" Harv grinned.

Anna smiled briefly at Harvey, then looked back to Joe. "*Mammi* wants you two to come for supper."

Harv shot Anna a knowing look. "Just *Mammi*, huh?"

Anna blushed.

Joe scratched the stubbles on his chin. He'd need to shave soon, so as not to offend *Mammi*. "I don't know if that's such a good idea," he said hesitantly.

"Well, my cousin Jacob is here and she thought it would be better if there were some other men that he could talk to. She'd be happy to have you," Anna said, then ducked her head. "And, uh, I would too."

That's all Joe needed to hear. "Come on, Harv, let's go."

"Ah man, I was just about to beat you," Harv said, folding his cards on the table.

"That's *your* version. We *both* know who was ahead." Joe smiled, catching Anna's eye. "That is, if you weren't trying to cheat again."

"I told you that I don't never cheat," Harv protested.

Joe raised his eyebrows, his doubtful expression evident.

"Well, okay. There was that one time, but –"

"We got people waitin' on us, Harv."

Harvey lowered his head sheepishly and bundled up in the jacket and scarf Anna had given him.

Joseph patiently waited for his old friend, then they followed Anna to the main house. When they arrived, Anna's family was already seated at the supper table.

FIFTEEN

*A*nna quickly moved to introduce everybody. She looked from Harvey and Joe to her cousin and his wife. "Harvey, Joe, this is my cousin Jacob and his wife Rachel and their three *kinner*: Leah, Kate, and Faithy."

"Well, if those aren't the three pertiest little girls I've ever seen!" Harvey gushed.

Anna watched as the girls' faces lit up. It seemed everyone loved Harv.

Jacob's eyes widened when he shook Joe's hand, as a look of recognition registered. "Joseph? Joseph Bender? I can't believe it's you!" He reached for his old friend to embrace him. "Jake Schrock, remember?"

Anna's mouth hung open. *Bender?*

Joe nodded to Jacob, then briefly glanced at Anna. "How have you been?"

"Wonderful, as you can see by my beautiful *fraa* and *kinner*. How about you? What are you doing in Pennsylvania? Did you finally get tired of old Bishop Burkholder?" Jake asked with a chuckle.

Mammi gasped.

"Trust me, *Mammi*, if you only knew him." Jacob clarified, "Strictest bishop I ever heard of."

"We shouldn't speak disrespectfully about our elders," *Mammi* reminded with a pointed glare. "No matter how strict they are."

Jacob ducked his head in apology. "Sorry."

Harvey spoke up unabashedly. "Well, I can't see no reason not to start eatin'."

As Jacob said the silent prayer, Anna couldn't help but dwell on Joe. So many questions filled her mind. She wished she could request a private audience with Joe – or Joseph – right this instant. He was Amish? Why hadn't he ever mentioned it to her?

She now realized that she really didn't know him at all. At least, not like she thought she did. No wonder he had so much character. She should have recognized it right away. As she thought on it, things finally began to add up. Like how he knew exactly how to handle a horse and buggy. Or that he was familiar with yumasetta and loved whoopie pies.

Apparently, the fact that he was homeless had thrown her for a loop. Which led her to another question: where was his family? And how did he end up on the streets?

How many secrets does Joseph Bender have? She wondered as she eyed him from across the table.

Even so, Anna couldn't help the excitement that built up inside her. Perhaps there was a chance for her and Joe. It almost seemed too good to be true. *Joe is Amish!*

This is exactly what I didn't need, Joseph thought. Not that he wasn't happy to see Jacob. No, that part was wonderful. But now Anna knew that he'd once been Amish. No doubt, by the curious way she was looking at him at present, Anna would want to know the truth of his past. All of it. He wasn't certain he was ready to share, but some things in life seemed to be inevitable.

After the dinner dishes had been washed, and the others had gone to bed, Anna beckoned Joe to the kitchen table. All was quiet in the house except for the fire crackling in the woodstove.

"Would you like more coffee?" Anna offered.

"No, thank you." He studied her as she took the seat opposite him. Joe waited patiently for Anna to express herself. He knew she must have a plethora of questions.

"How come you never told me?"

He shrugged. "There's nothing to tell. I used to be Amish, I'm not anymore."

"You make a horrible liar, Joseph Bender." Anna's reproving eyes met his.

Joe sighed. "Where do you want me to start?"

Anna reached for his hands and clasped them in her own. "How about the beginning?"

Joseph nodded, then began his story.

"I don't know if you ever heard the controversy about the orange safety triangles?" He lifted his eyes in question.

Anna nodded. "That was Swartzentruber Amish, right?

Joe offered an affirmative nod. "Well, I guess it kind of started with that. I'd put one on my buggy, but they were *verboten*. The bishop and elders had decided that we, as a district, weren't going to conform to the world. That meant no orange safety triangles.

"Anyway, that was what put me on the black list the first time. The second time was Mary, she was my *aldi*." Joseph searched Anna's eyes to see whether she'd want him to continue or not.

Anna bade him on.

"Mary and I had been courting for a while. She was a quiet type and didn't share her thoughts much, but I was fine with that. I figured that if she had something to say, she'd say it. Well, one night, I'd gone to her bedroom like I usually did." Joe stopped when Anna's eyes widened. "I'm sorry, but this is necessary if you want to know the whole story."

"Did you..." Anna's voiced stopped short of asking the question he knew was on her mind.

Joe shook his head. "No, I respected Mary. I wouldn't...I mean, I was certainly tempted to, but no. We never had a physical relationship."

He watched as Anna released a nervous sigh.

"They do allow bed courtship in my old district." Joseph continued, "Anyway, this particular time I'd gone into her room, Mary's brother was there. I'll never forget the look on Mary's face. It was a mixture of embarrassment and fear. Anna, Mary's brother was defiling her." It hurt to say the words and his blood still boiled at the thought. "I was so shocked and angry. In hopes of her brother changing his behavior, I told him we were betrothed and that we'd be married in six months. Do you know what he said to me?"

Anna shook her head and he noticed tears in her eyes.

"He smirked and said, 'Well, I guess that means I still get six months with her.' If I ever thought I might be able to take someone's life, it was then. It took every ounce of composure I had not to strike Mary's brother. But I knew that if I allowed myself the pleasure, my anger would become insatiable and I'd kill the man.

"Mary was embarrassed. She didn't want me to go to the bishop, but I had to. I thought that surely something would be done about it. From there, it seemed like things just got worse. Sure, the elders ordered her brother not to go near her, but do you think he listened?

"I finally took matters into my own hands. I think Mary hated me for it, but I just couldn't stand by and see her being taken advantage of. I went to the *Englisch* authorities. At first, they didn't want to do anything either. It seemed like they were real wary of getting involved in Amish matters. But I kept bugging them about it until they could no longer ignore me. I desperately wanted to see her brother put behind bars so he wouldn't hurt Mary or anyone else again.

"I tried to keep Mary away from the house as much as possible, so we'd go riding in my buggy a lot. Well, one night when we were out on the highway a car came around the corner. He wasn't going too fast, but he'd said that he just didn't see the buggy. I know he would have seen us if I'd had the orange triangle on my buggy, I'm almost certain of it.

"Anna," Joe took a deep breath. "Mary died in that accident. We were so close to going to court, but the case ended up being dismissed because Mary was no longer there to testify.

"Do you know who the elders were angry with? Me. Do you know who ended up being excommunicated over this whole matter? Me. They said I could be accepted back into the fold if I repented. If *I* repented? No way. I wasn't going to do it."

Tears now streamed from Anna's eyes and pooled on the table in front of her. "Oh, Joe. I'm so sorry. What they did was wrong."

"Now, you and I can't be together because of it." Joseph wiped his frustrated tears on the sleeve of his shirt.

Anna shook her head. "Our bishop is different. We are not Swartzentruber, we are much faster."

Joe's mouth lifted a little on one side. "I noticed."

"I'm certain that if you tell the story to Bishop Hostettler, he'll understand. I don't think he'll uphold the *Bann*."

Joe sensed Anna's excitement, but he didn't want to get her hopes up. "I don't know, Anna." Joseph's face then brightened as though lightning suddenly struck. "Does this mean you want to be with me now – that we can date?"

Anna nodded.

Joe stood up from the table and moved around to Anna's side. Anna stood to meet him and he pulled her into his embrace. He gently stroked her back and held her tight for several minutes. He never thought he'd be given this opportunity again. "I might want to kiss you," he admitted.

She smiled up at him and replied, "I might want to kiss you back."

That was all the invitation he needed. Joseph bent his head and brought his eager lips to Anna's. Only in his dreams had he ever believed this would happen, but here was Anna, in his arms. He couldn't help but breathe a silent prayer of thanks for God's providence once again.

SIXTEEN

*A*nna couldn't erase the smile from her lips. She'd dreamt again last night. It was the same dream she'd had before, but this time she recognized the man's face. It was clearly Joseph's. Chills had traveled up her spine and arms the second she awoke. And now, as she tried to concentrate on the customers in the store, they'd returned. She felt so giddy, as though she could run out into the snow and turn cartwheels.

Joe had dropped her off this morning and said he had errands to run in town again. This time she'd agreed to have lunch with him. She did wonder what business he had in town, but she didn't want to be nosy. She'd asked a couple of questions, but all his answers had been vague. It seemed Joseph still held some secrets he was not willing to reveal.

Anna glanced around the store. *Where did all these people come from?* There had to be at least twice as many as yesterday.

"Excuse me, Ma'am."

Anna looked up at the forty-something *Englisch* woman in front of her. "May I help you?"

The woman nodded and pointed to *Mammi's* Christmas quilt. "Is that one of the quilts that will be discounted during your After-Thanksgiving Sale?"

With a puzzled look, Anna asked, "After-Thanksgiving Sale? I'm sorry, I don't know what –"

Linda quickly approached. "Anna, I'm sorry to interrupt but will you go help the customers over in the corner? They're asking questions about your faceless Amish dolls and I thought you could answer them more accurately than I can, since you make them."

"Yes, but this woman was asking about a Thanksgiving Sale?" Anna referred the lady to Linda.

"After-Thanksgiving Sale," the customer corrected. "I was wondering if that quilt was going to be on sale."

Linda shooed Anna away to help the other customers while she waited on the woman. Anna wondered what After-Thanksgiving Sale the lady had been talking about. She hadn't heard anything about a sale from Linda. No doubt the lady probably got them mixed up with one of the other stores in town that participated in some Black Friday sale. But they'd never participated in that madness.

Anna glanced up at the clock and noticed it was almost noon. Where had the day gone? She approached the other customers near her handmade dolls. "May I help you?"

"Are you the one who makes these adorable little dolls?" a woman asked.

"Yes."

"I see you only have four here. Do you have any more in the back?"

"No. That is all we have available," Anna replied apologetically. "But I could make more if you need them."

"I was hoping to purchase a set for each of my granddaughters. I'll need at least five sets." The woman smiled. "Can you make them with blue and green clothes? Those are my favorites."

Anna mentally counted how long it would take her to make them. "When do you need them?"

"I'll need them for Christmas, but I'd rather not wait until the last minute." The woman opened up her purse and pulled out her cell phone. Anna waited patiently while watching the lady tap the phone's screen several times. "My calendar," the woman explained. "Is two weeks enough time?"

"Two weeks will be fine."

"That's wonderful. Where do I pay for them?"

Anna looked up to see Joe standing at the register ringing up customers. She smiled and walked the customer over to the counter. "This man here can help you."

Joseph winked at Anna. "Linda put me to work. I guess we can do lunch later, *jah*?"

Anna smiled at Joe's use of Pennsylvania Deitsh. It seemed he'd been speaking it more lately and it warmed Anna's heart. "*Jah*."

"It looks like more customers just walked in. You'd better go help them," he suggested, while receiving the customer's payment.

Anna nodded and walked toward another group of inquisitive patrons. *This is crazy! I've never seen so many people in here before.*

"Whew! I thought the customers would never stop coming," Anna said as she took a seat next to Joe behind the sales counter.

Linda rotated the key in the lock and finally turned the sign to CLOSED, thirty minutes after normal closing time. "I think that was the best day we've ever had!" Linda said enthusiastically.

Joe winked at Linda behind Anna's back. "Just wait until the After-Thanksgiving Sale. I bet we get even more customers."

"Whoever had the idea to come up with that was brilliant," Anna smiled.

Linda's eyes widened. "Oh, Anna, I didn't tell you. Your grandmother's quilt sold."

"It did? Really?" Anna glanced over at the quilt still hanging in the window. "Why is it still here then?"

"The lady already paid for it, but she won't pick it up until Friday. She didn't want to take the chance of missing it. I went ahead and gave her the sale price," Linda said.

"Sale price? What is the sale price?" A worried frown crossed Anna's brow.

"Six hundred-fifty dollars." Linda smiled.

Anna's jaw dropped. "What? That's the *sale* price? But that's more than what we were asking for in the first place!"

Joe perked up and smiled. "Go look at the tag."

Anna rushed to the quilt and turned the paper hang tag around. "This says Thirteen hundred dollars!" Anna looked at Linda in confusion. "I don't understand."

Linda began, "I had a marketing genius come into the store a while back. He offered to do a free promotion for me. When he looked at the items in our store, he noticed many of them were underpriced. The gentleman agreed to do some research and price our items according to our competitors' prices."

"But we don't have any competitors," Anna reasoned.

"We do online. Quilts like your grandmother's sell for up to two thousand dollars, so six hundred dollars is a really good deal." Linda glanced down at the clipboard in her hand. "Which reminds me. You said your grandmother has more quilts, right?"

Anna nodded.

"We're going to need them," Linda said. "Can you bring in at least four?"

Anna's brow shot up. "Do you think we might sell that many?"

"Who knows? But I'd like to be prepared just in case."

Joe piped in. "I think that's a good idea."

Linda turned to Joe. "Do you think you can come back and work on Friday? We're going to need all the help we can get. Besides, I think the female customers enjoy seeing a man in the store. I can tell Anna does," she teased.

A beautiful blush darkened Anna's cheeks when she caught Joe's smile.

"We'd better get home, Anna. We don't want your grandmother to worry," Joe warned.

"Can you two come in an hour early on Friday? I'd like to rearrange the store a little bit and find places for your grandmother's quilts," Linda requested.

"*Jah*," Anna agreed. "I can't wait to tell *Mammi* about her Christmas quilt!"

SEVENTEEN

*A*aron opened the wooden cabinet above the bathroom sink and removed the small hand mirror. It was essential that he look his very best tonight if he stood any chance of getting Anna back. After determining he hadn't missed any stray facial hairs with his razor, he ran a comb through his locks to be sure they weren't unruly.

He thought of his visit to Anna's yesterday. Her cousin Jacob seemed pretty nice and didn't balk at allowing him to help around the farm. They'd had a very valuable conversation, Aaron had thought. However, he was extremely disappointed to hear that Anna had taken in not one, but two loathsome beggars. How dare those grown men take advantage of two single women who were scarcely making it themselves. Anna and her grandmother didn't need two extra mouths to feed, especially with Anna's cousin visiting.

In learning of his real name, which Jacob unwittingly volunteered, Aaron had uncovered some pretty interesting facts about Anna's favorite homeless man. He would be none too happy to share them with her. Aaron couldn't wait to see the look on the loser's face when he divulged his information in front of Anna's family. Surely, he knew far more about Joseph Bender and his past than Anna was aware of.

Aaron came up with a plan last night after combing the internet at the library all afternoon. He had a trick or two up his sleeve – hopefully, ones that would present himself as the hero once Bender was out of the picture for good.

He had the feeling that *Mammi* was going to try to deter him from coming today, so he was sure to tell her how much he was looking forward to it. He praised her cooking abilities and offered to do several chores around the house just so she wouldn't have the heart to tell him not to come. Thankfully, it must've worked because Anna's grandmother had kept mute on the subject, although he sensed her discomfort when he mentioned that he'd be seeing her when he returned for Thanksgiving dinner. He wasn't bothered by it, though.

No, the thought of seeing Joseph Bender squirm under Anna's watchful eye would be all the satisfaction he needed. A slow smirk slithered across Aaron's clean-shaven face.

When dinner preparations were well underway, Anna beckoned *Mammi* to the spare bedroom where she'd moved her quilting frame. She didn't want to forget to bring more quilts to the shop tomorrow as Linda had suggested. Just the thought of selling *one* more quilt thrilled Anna to the bone; she couldn't imagine selling several in one day. The sale from *Mammi's* Christmas quilt along with her normal paycheck would be enough to cover their mortgage payment this month, but it would still leave them short on the property tax bill. But like *Mammi* said, God would provide for them somehow.

Anna stepped into the room and looked around. Something didn't seem right.

Mammi gasped. "Some of my quilts are missing! I had at least three more in here." She moved the plastic covered quilts, in an effort to locate the missing blankets.

"Do you think Jacob may have used them? Maybe the *kinner* got cold last night," Anna suggested.

"He didn't mention it, but I guess it's possible. I'll ask him later. Right now, we need to figure out which quilts you're taking to sell and get back to that dinner before it burns."

Anna took four various quilts from *Mammi's* limited repertoire. "Don't worry, *Mammi*. I'm sure there's a logical explanation for your missing quilts."

Mammi's disappointed countenance lifted some. "You're probably right, dear."

Anna quickly placed the quilts upstairs in her bedroom and glanced out her window. She groaned when she spotted Aaron's buggy driving up the lane. She hurried down to chat with *Mammi*.

"*Mammi*, I thought you were going to tell Aaron not to come," Anna said in exasperation.

"I'm sorry, dear. I just couldn't tell that boy no. He seemed so eager to come," *Mammi* explained.

"*Mammi*, you know Joseph and I..." Anna stopped mid-sentence, reconsidering her words. "I'm not interested in Aaron anymore. I thought I'd already made that clear." Just the fact that *Mammi* knew *anything* about her love life frustrated Anna. It wasn't their traditional way of doing things. Of course, Aaron was the one to blame for that. If he hadn't come to visit often and only courted her during singings and such, their prior relationship would have most likely gone undetected by *Mammi*.

How is Joe going to respond to Aaron's presence? Anna remembered the last time they'd seen each other and a smile crept across her features. Neither Aaron, Joe, nor even herself for that matter, had any clue that she was going to kiss Joseph that night. She could only imagine what Aaron had said to Joe after she'd gone inside.

One thing she realized about Joseph was that he was strong in presence of mind – and honest. Those were two qualities she could admire in a man.

Or perhaps a husband?

Joseph spotted Anna through the window he'd just finished cleaning and tapped it to get her attention. Anna's countenance lit up at the sight of him and it warmed Joe's heart. What made him so deserving of such a wonderful woman? *Nothing*, he'd thought. It had to be God – there was no other explanation for it.

Anna rounded the corner of the house and came to meet him. "Hey." She smiled in greeting.

"It's too cold for you to be out here without a jacket." He opened his own jacket and spread out his arms. "Come," he invited.

Anna came close and slid her arms around his back inside his jacket. Fortunately they were in a place where no one could see. Joseph held her tight and gave thanks once again.

"I forgot to tell you," Anna said. "Aaron's here."

"I know. I saw him pull up. I plan to go tell him hello as soon as I'm done kissing you." He raised his eyebrows and grinned.

"Oh?"

Joe smiled and brought his lips to hers, the frosty air rising between them. He released her from his embrace before things heated up a little too much. "Thank you for letting me steal a kiss or two."

"Oh no, those were freely given," she admitted, biting her bottom lip.

"Yeah? And can I expect a few more later?"

Anna had never seemed more beautiful. "Maybe." She winked before turning the corner of the house and disappeared from Joe's sight.

Joseph released a puff of frigid air and could have jumped for joy, he was so exhilarated. Having Anna as his *aldi* was like a dream come true. If he didn't rein in his thoughts, though, he and Anna would be married with *kinner* in no time.

But he couldn't think that way. If he'd learned anything by Mary's death, it was to not assume anything. Only God knew what the future held. And as difficult as it seemed, Joseph realized he must trust God. What if something happened to Anna? What if it didn't work out between them?

"She's a good kisser, huh?" Aaron's voice echoed from the opposite corner of the house that Anna had just turned. He walked confidently toward Joseph.

Joe frowned. "What were you doing watching us? It was a private moment."

"Private? If you want private, I suggest a room. A bedroom, perhaps? Anna does have a mighty fine figure, wouldn't you say?"

Joseph couldn't help it when his fist met with Aaron's jaw. At least that's what he told himself. After doing nothing when Mary's brother taunted him, and her dying without receiving due justice, he'd decided he would never tolerate someone disrespecting the woman he loved again. There were just some things he couldn't – and wouldn't – stand for.

Aaron sneered and wiped a drop of blood from his lip. "Perfect. That's exactly what I was hoping for." He passed Joseph, purposely bumping his shoulder in the process, and moved toward the back door.

EIGHTEEN

*A*nna hadn't been happy when she heard that Joe punched Aaron. It certainly didn't win him any favor with *Mammi*. As a matter of fact, *Mammi* had mentioned privately to Anna that she thought it might be better if Joseph and Harvey left.

Why had he done it? She'd asked Joe and he refused to explain, except that he had good reason. Was there ever a good reason to use violence? This certainly would not help his standing in the Amish community either. Frustration mounted as Anna took a bite of her turkey dinner. This was anything but the Thanksgiving she had anticipated.

Aaron glanced at Anna across the table. So far, it looked as if his plan was taking shape nicely. She was mad. And not at him – at that vagrant. Aaron appeared casual, but inside he was bursting with joy. Just wait until his next revelation.

Joseph Bender would be falling so hard, he won't even know what hit him.

Joseph thought of leaving the dinner early, but Jake insisted he stay for dessert and games. For his friend's sake, he would. But Anna's disapproval cut him to the heart. Why didn't she trust him? Should he have to explain his actions to her? Wasn't his word good enough?

He and Jake now played chess while Harvey challenged Aaron to game of gin rummy. The ladies sat at the kitchen table talking and minding the *kinner*.

"How have things been at the fabric shop, Anna?" Aaron asked, grating on Joe's nerves further.

"Oh, they've been great!" she answered cheerfully.

"Have *Mammi's* quilts sold? I know you were talking about her Christmas quilt the last time we were together," Aaron asked warmly. Joseph knew he was doing this just to get to him...and to Anna, but in a different way. Joe didn't appreciate his blatant audacity.

Anna's face lit up. "Oh yes! We sold her Christmas quilt yesterday. I was meaning to give you back that money you lent us." Anna walked to her purse, which she kept on the sideboard.

"Oh no. That wasn't a loan. You don't need to repay it," Aaron insisted.

"I feel like I should, besides..." A frown quickly crossed Anna's face as she searched through her wallet. "*Mammi*, did you take any of the money from my wallet?"

Mammi's face crinkled. "No. Haven't touched it."

"But there was over five hundred dollars in here," Anna exclaimed. "Now there's only two hundred." She helplessly looked around at each of them. "Joe? You remember, right? You watched me put the money in my wallet at the store."

"Yep," Joe agreed. "Linda gave you five-fifty for the quilt."

Aaron stood up and moved to where Anna stood. He whispered something in her ear and Anna shook her head in disbelief. He finally spoke aloud, "It wonders me if maybe good old Joseph didn't take it. Beggars are always in need of extra cash. Three hundred dollars is a nice little sum of money for someone who has *nothing*." He looked at *Mammi* to gather sympathy and possibly even support.

Joe stood up and challenged him. "That's ridiculous! Anna knows I'm not a thief." He looked to Anna whose confidence in him appeared to be dwindling by the minute.

"Isn't it kind of a coincidence that Joseph knew Anna had that money in her wallet?" Aaron goaded.

"Aaron, stop," Anna demanded. "Joe didn't take the money."

"Are you certain? I bet he's got it in his pocket right now – or maybe he's stashing it in his room," Aaron accused. "I have an idea. Why don't we check?"

"Go ahead," Joe uttered between gritted teeth. Joseph's face darkened in humiliation. How dare this jerk come in here and accuse him of thievery. Now, he wished he'd hit him harder. Aaron's handsome looks certainly didn't match his insufferable personality. If he'd broken his nose, they'd probably be equal.

Mammi spoke up. "I think that might be a good idea, Anna." Joe didn't take offense at *Mammi's* words. He couldn't blame Anna's grandmother for being overly cautious.

Joe nodded in permission. "My pants don't have pockets. You may check my jacket; it's hanging by the door."

A worried frown crossed Anna's face and Harvey, Jacob, and his family minded their own business. No doubt Harv knew what Aaron was up to and Joe was certain it was difficult for him to hold his piece.

"Is this really necessary?" Anna protested.

"It's okay, Anna," Joe assured. "I don't have anything to hide."

Aaron smirked at Joe and raised an eyebrow. "Don't you?"

Anna looked from Aaron to Joseph in confusion.

"Nothing in his jacket," Aaron admitted. "But we'd better check his room, just to be sure. It would be terrible if you had a thief living amongst you." Aaron looked sympathetically at *Mammi.*

Harvey and Jake now stood up. Harv couldn't hold his tongue any longer, it seemed. "You have a lot of nerve, young man."

"I'm not the only one," Aaron retorted. "I bet Joe's got it in his room. Unless you're a thief too, old man."

"That's uncalled for," Jacob now spoke.

Aaron marched toward the door. "Who's coming with me?"

Joe, Anna, *Mammi*, and Harv followed him out. Joseph opened the door to the *dawdi haus* and allowed Aaron to roam around, poking through their stuff. Everyone stood by the door and watched as though a scene from a movie played before their eyes. Joe knew that if he just kept his mouth closed, Aaron would prove himself the fool he was.

After probing the small main room, Aaron opened the door to the bedroom Joseph slept in. He opened up a few drawers of the bureau, finding nothing, as Joe knew he would. Aaron then walked over to the nightstand and opened the top drawer. He pulled out the Bible Joe had been reading. Aaron haphazardly thumbed through the pages when something green fell to the floor. "Well, look what we've got here." Aaron bent down and picked up some folded bills. "Anna, I do believe this is your three hundred dollars." He handed the bills to Anna.

Anna looked forlornly at Joseph as she counted the bills.

Joe's mouth hung open, but he finally found his voice. "Anna, I swear –"

Mammi's gasp cut off Joe's protests. "My quilts!" She pointed under the bed. "Anna, my missing quilts!"

The disillusioned look Anna gave Joe gripped his heart. He watched as her eyes filled with tears. She'd clearly lost all faith in him.

"Anna, please. I can explain that later –" Joe began helplessly.

"Wait!" Aaron declared. "It gets better. Anna, did you know that Joseph Bender is, indeed, a crook? I did a little research on him, you see. He used to be some company big shot. He went to jail for cheating thousands of people out of their money. Your Joe stole millions of dollars."

"It's not true," Joseph insisted.

Aaron pulled several papers out of his jacket and handed them to Anna. "Let her judge for herself who the liar is here."

Anna burst out of the *dawdi haus* with hot tears pouring from her eyes. How could she have been so wrong about Joe? She truly had no clue who Joseph Bender was. What had she been thinking to bring him into her home? And worse still, into her heart.

Upon entering the main house, she excused herself and ran upstairs to her room. *Why God? Why did you bring Joseph into my life just to have him take advantage of me and Mammi?* She didn't want to believe it was true, but how could there be any other explanation?

She unfolded the papers Aaron had given her and read the words on the page. Every one of them. The truth stared back at her in black and white. There was even a picture of Joe in a fancy *Englisch* suit. Then there was a picture of him in an orange prison jumper. The article detailed how he hired clients, contributed to their success, and made them millions of dollars. Then stole it.

Joseph...not only a robber of worldly goods, but a thief of the heart as well. Just when she'd thought she finally found *the one*. Anna sobbed into her palms, blurring the words on the page in her lap.

Anna lifted her head at the sound of a gentle knock on the door. She reluctantly shuffled to the door and twisted the knob. Aaron stood in the doorway, an apologetic look on his face.

"Anna, I'm so sorry," he offered. "I didn't mean for that to get out of hand."

She brushed away her tears and sniffled, afraid to speak lest the tears begin falling again.

Aaron spoke tenderly. "When I found out that Joseph Bender was a crook, I knew I couldn't let him fool you any longer. I knew that even if it hurt you, he must be called on the carpet." He shook his head. "I hope you realize that my intention was not to hurt you. I'd never want to do that."

Anna didn't know what to make of Aaron's words. She nodded in understanding.

"Listen, whatever happens between us doesn't really matter. I just didn't want to see you with the likes of someone like Joseph Bender. I hope we can still be friends."

This was a side of Aaron she hadn't seen often. Perhaps she hadn't given him enough of a chance. This whole time he'd just been trying to protect her, she realized.

J. E. B. Spredemann

Anna studied Aaron. He'd offered her marriage and she'd turned him down. Now he simply offered friendship.

Aaron ducked his head, dismissing himself from the room. She heard his heavy footsteps on the wooden stairs.

Aaron really is a good man. Perhaps she should reconsider his proposal. Maybe she'd been too hasty and misjudged him.

But what of Joe?

Anna shoved the papers into her dresser drawer, willing herself to forget about Joseph Bender. Tomorrow she would ask Jacob to ask Joe and Harv to leave the property. She didn't know where they would go, but it wasn't her concern. They were grown men, they could take care of themselves.

A pang shot through Anna's heart. She'd thought they'd been genuine friends. How wrong she was. She was beginning to realize she was a very poor judge of character. Everything she'd believed about Joe had been wrong. And everything she'd believed about Aaron was wrong too.

Anna took a deep breath and realized what she needed to do. She must go and apologize to Aaron. Perhaps he'd forgive her and they could start all over again.

One thing was certain: she had to do everything possible to forget Joseph Bender. But for the life of her, she couldn't figure how she could take him out of her dreams. Or remove the pain that plagued her heart.

NINETEEN

Joe lit the end of his cigarette, sat down on his crate in the alley, inhaled deeply, then blew out a breath of toxic smoke.

"Joe, that's your third one in a row. I think you need to take it easy," Harv warned. "Besides, you should be turning to God in your time of need."

Joseph released a sarcastic laugh. "God? This is a classic example of what happens when I start trusting in your God, Harv. I'm done." He pulled a small glass bottle from his pocket, unscrewed the lid, and brought it to his lips.

Harvey quickly knocked the bottle out of his hands. "What are you doin', Joe? You can't drink that stuff."

Joe frowned at Harv. "What'd you do that for?" He walked over to the bottle and picked it up out of the snow. After determining it was now empty, he threw the bottle at the brick wall, hollering a curse word in frustration.

"Why don't you fight for her?"

"What?"

"Fight. If you truly are innocent, why don't you prove it to her? Show her the articles Mr. Perfect purposely ignored in order to dig out the trash."

"It's too late, Harvey. Linda told me that she's engaged now. Besides, Anna believed what she *wanted* to. Probably wouldn't believe me even if I proved the truth to her."

"Balderdash! She can't be engaged. It's only been four days. My, that scum sure does work fast," Harv said disgustedly.

"Well, she chose him." Joe shrugged.

"No. She chose you. And I don't know why you allow her to believe a lie." Harvey sighed. "Do you really want Miss Anna to marry that jerk?"

Footsteps crunching through the snow drew their attention to the opening of the alley, interrupting their conversation. Joe was pleased to see Linda. It seemed she'd been a true friend and had given him the benefit of the doubt.

"Joe, I need your help," she requested.

"Sure, Linda. What do you need?"

"Will you come back to the store with me?"

Joe's eyebrows raised. "Is Anna there? Because if she is, I'd rather not."

"No. She's on lunch right now. Aaron picked her up."

Joe rolled his eyes. *It figures.* "Okay." He glanced at Harv for approval.

"Don't mind me. I'll be fine here," Harvey insisted.

"If it begins snowing, you come to the store," Linda said. "I have a small back storage room the two of you can share when the weather is foul. It's not much, but at least it'll be shelter."

Joe touched Linda's arm. "Thank you, Linda. You truly are a kind person."

Her concerned eyes met his. "Anna is too."

Joe nodded, then followed after Linda to Threads of Beauty. She led him to the backroom and detailed what she wanted done after hours. He also had extra time to finish up the project Linda had commissioned this morning, several hours prior to Anna's arrival.

"Is it working now?" Linda asked hopefully.

"Yep. Should be working like a charm."

"I want to pay you for the work you've been doing for me." Linda opened her wallet and handed Joseph a few bills.

"Thank you." Joe took one of the bills and stuffed it in his pocket. He handed the others back to her. "Will you add the extra to Anna's check, please?"

Linda's eyes showed empathy. "Of course."

"But please, don't let her know."

Linda nodded in understanding. The front bell rang, alerting her to a customer's presence. She and Joseph walked to the front store and she glanced down at her watch. "It's already ten minutes after one and Anna's not back yet. Where could she be?" A group of patrons poured in at once when Linda noticed a tour bus outside. "Oh boy. Joe, will you please stay and help me? I can't possibly assist all these customers myself."

"Sure. What would you have me do?"

"Just run the cash register."

Joe took his place behind the counter and began ringing up a customer's purchase, while Linda met the other customers' needs. *Where is Anna?* Joe glanced at the clock on the wall which revealed it was now twenty minutes after one.

Five minutes later, a smiling Anna waltzed through the door with Aaron in tow. She glanced at Joe and frowned, then looked up at the clock. Her eyes widened and she covered her mouth, most likely realizing her tardiness. Fortunately, the store had cleared out by now.

Good. Now that she'd returned, Joe could go. He summoned Linda to the cash register and told her of his intentions.

"Will you hold on just a little bit? I'd like to have a chat with Anna in the back before you leave," Linda requested.

"Sure."

Linda turned to Anna, who'd been showing one of *Mammi's* quilts to Aaron. The fact that they'd sold three over the last few days hadn't surprised Joseph at all. Linda realized the man knew what he was doing. He was very good at what he did. It's too bad Anna couldn't see Joe's worth.

"Anna, I'd like to have a word with you in the back, please," Linda requested.

Anna nodded sheepishly and sent Aaron a fleeting glance. Aaron nodded back. Anna followed her employer to the back room.

"I don't think I have to tell you that you're nearly a half-hour late."

"I'm sorry, Linda. We lost track of time." Anna explained further, "Aaron took me to his home for lunch and it took longer than I'd thought."

"I've decided to hire Joe as a second employee," Linda stated. "He's proved valuable many times and he's a good worker."

"I don't think that's such a good idea." Anna frowned. "Since they've been gone, other things have come up missing at our place too."

"Nevertheless, he's now an employee of Threads of Beauty." Linda just hoped that Joe would agree to it now. With the extra money they'd been bringing in of late, she could afford to hire him at least part-time. Linda walked to the door and beckoned Joseph.

Apparently, Joe and Aaron had been in some sort of discussion, because Joe's arms were crossed over his chest and his countenance reflected frustration. He walked to the door, leaving Aaron standing near the counter alone. Linda wished Anna's fiancé would leave, but she wouldn't be rude by asking him to.

Joseph walked in with the door clicking shut behind him. "You wanted to see me?" He kept his gaze steady on Linda and she knew it was to avoid eye contact with Anna. Linda thought Joe and Anna had made a cute couple.

"Yes. I just informed Anna that I hired you part-time," Linda stated.

Joe glanced nervously at Anna. "Uh, you did?"

Linda nodded in affirmation. "I'd like you to stay until closing today, if you can."

"If you think you need me."

"There's always stuff to do back here if there aren't any customers up front," Linda explained. She turned to Anna. "You may go back up front."

Anna nodded and walked back to the main store, with not so much as a glance at Joe.

Linda hoped she was doing the right thing. After Anna disappeared, she turned back to Joe. "I haven't said anything to Anna about your private activities. She doesn't need to know anything about that."

"I appreciate that, Linda."

"Why don't you work on getting that back storage room cleaned out so you and Harvey will have some shelter?"

Joe nodded.

"I'm just sorry I can't offer you more."

"Oh no, Linda. You've been a great help to me and Harv. We'll never forget it."

"Well, you've more than earned it. You've really helped Threads of Beauty get on its feet." Linda smiled at Joe, but his reciprocating grin was nothing like it had been when he and

Anna were dating. It seemed as though a dark cloud hovered over him. Seeing Anna with Aaron must be difficult for Joseph, she realized. Perhaps the two of them working together would change that.

TWENTY

o, no, no! Anna's heart cried out when she heard that she'd be working with Joe. How was she ever going to get over him if she had to see him every day? She yearned to forget the electrified feeling the air took on when they were in the same room, or what it felt like to be enveloped in his loving embrace, or how his soft lips moved on hers. How would her heart ever mend?

But he's a liar and a thief, she reminded herself. The reason they weren't together anymore. She'd since replayed every conversation they'd had in her mind, questioning the validity of each one. Had he made those stories up? Did he truly save Harvey from alcoholism? Was there really ever a Mary?

She glanced out the window watching as Joe now lit up a cigarette. *Jah,* she was better off without a man like that. Aaron was right, she didn't want to find herself a couple of years down the road married to a lazy drunk. He'd also pointed out that Joe was prone to violence, citing his busted lip as an example. Not that she'd ever seen Joe drink, nor did he appear slothful.

The worst part about the whole thing, though, was Joe wouldn't even look her in the eye. Every time she glanced his way, he'd abruptly look away. She supposed it was embarrassment, or perhaps shame that caused him to do so. It wasn't as though she hated him or anything. No, she just couldn't trust him is all. And wasn't trust the foundation of any healthy relationship?

"Miss?"

Anna had been staring out the window at Joe so long, she hadn't even realized a customer had been in the store. She shook her head in an attempt to dispel her thoughts. If she didn't pull herself together, Linda was going to end up firing her. And there was no way she could afford for that to happen.

It felt good to somewhat get back on his feet, Joseph realized. With a part-time job, at least he was able to buy some food for him and Harv. Who knows? Maybe he'd even be able to save up enough to rent a place of their own by next year. But as long as Anna was still living alone with *Mammi*, he resolved to have Linda keep a portion of his paycheck for Anna. She needed it more than he did.

When the other businesses in town noticed the recent success of Threads of Beauty, they began asking Linda questions. She'd shared with them the secret of her success: she'd hired a marketing consultant. She hadn't given out Joe's name, but she had asked his permission to do so. He was certain he could make a good living as a professional marketing consultant. But he'd declined.

The problem was, he wasn't ready for Anna to find out. Not that it would make a difference in their non-existent relationship. Despite Anna's poor choice of a partner, Joe still cared for her deeply. Perhaps he was a fool to ever think he'd had chance with her in the first place. Anna had just seemed so different than everybody else. Hadn't she exhibited her kindheartedness when she'd brought food to him and Harv in the alley? Why, then, did she seem so callous toward him now? It just wasn't like her, at least not the Anna he'd known.

"Whatcha thinkin' about?" Harvey popped up from his little cot in the small storage room they were sharing.

"What else?" Joe rolled his eyes.

"Ah…Miss Anna." Harv nodded. A strand of gray hair stuck up from his head, reminding Joe that they should both be asleep by now.

"Is the light bothering you?"

"No. You know me, I can sleep through anything. But don't you think *you* should get some sleep? It's after two. Before you know it you'll need to get up for work."

Joseph sighed. "I know. I'm trying to figure out what to do."

"'Bout what?"

"Everything." Joe hung his head. "I'm contemplating leaving."

Harv's mouth hung open like the flap on a mailbox. "Leaving? But Joe…" Harvey sighed. "I guess you gotta do what ya gotta do, but I sure will miss you if ya go. Where ya goin'?"

"Don't know. I don't think I can stay here, though. Maybe I'll go to Paradise and see my friend Samuel. He was always real nice." Joe shrugged his shoulders non-committedly. "Probably has a wife and *kinner* by now like Jake."

"Why don't you go talk to your friend Jacob?"

"And chance running into Anna or Aaron? No, thank you."

"You only work part-time. You could go while she's still working." Harv glanced at Joseph who was shaking his head. "Why not? Oh, I get it. Your pride, right?"

"I feel like such a failure, Harv. It seems other guys my age have everything. And here I am, with no place of my own, in a tiny little room, living off the good graces of a woman. Oh yeah, but I do have a job! In a *fabric shop*," he said with more than a hint of cynicism.

"That's nothin' to be ashamed of. Everyone's gotta start somewhere." Harvey's sympathetic gaze rested on Joe's distraught countenance. "Listen to me, Joseph. A true friend is not going to care about all that. You are a good person."

"I don't know."

"Well, I do. And I think somewhere deep inside Anna knows it too."

Joseph reached over and turned out the light. "I'm going to sleep now."

"Will ya think on it, Joe?" Harvey's voice sounded in the darkness.

"Yeah, I'll think on it."

Aaron considered himself lucky...or perhaps a better term would be smart. He'd wanted Anna back, but he didn't think she'd be accepting his proposal right off the bat. Nor did he believe she'd ever agree to marry him this wedding season – January, to be exact – but she had.

But one problem still existed.

Joseph Bender.

He thought for sure that after he'd been kicked off the Smuckers' property, he'd be rid of him for good. Now Anna's boss had hired Joseph to work with Anna. Why any man would agree to working in a fabric shop was beyond his comprehension. Unless, of course, it was so he could gander at Anna all day. Aaron did not like that one bit.

Something had to be done, but what?

As long as Joseph Bender was around, Aaron considered him a threat. Anna still hadn't gazed at him with the same loving adoration he'd seen while she was in Joe's arms. And she certainly hadn't kissed him the way she had Joe. That fact alone irked him to no end.

He must find a way to get rid of Bender for good.

TWENTY-ONE

The more Anna worked with Joseph, the more she realized he was the Joe she'd always known. The fact that he was a thief still baffled her. He seemed so…so…normal. Honest. Not like someone who would take advantage of others. The one thing she'd loved about Joe in the first place was that he'd always been genuine. And respectful. And kind.

But he's a thief, she reminded herself. *You saw the money in his room, the missing quilts under his bed.* Anna sighed. Why couldn't she reconcile the two images of Joe? Probably because they were such a stark contrast. *Ach, I hate this!* She desired to believe the best about Joe. She wanted him to be good.

She glanced up from the cash register and studied Joe as he showed a customer one of the quilts. His eyes sparkled and his laugh carried across the store. She'd missed seeing that. She knew she would always remember with fondness the times she'd shared lunch with Joe and Harv in the alley. An ache crept across her heart once again. She'd lost two good friends.

The attractive young woman smiled back at Joseph and placed her hand on his forearm. *Does he know her?* Joe walked up to the sales counter with the woman and handed the quilt to Anna. Anna rang up the customer's purchase and placed it into a large bag.

Joe glanced up at the clock, then back at Anna. "Please let Linda know I'm taking an early lunch. I should be back in an hour." He smiled at the woman beside him and she slipped her hand into the crook of his arm. "Ready?" he asked.

The woman nodded happily.

Anna's mouth hung open as she watched Joseph walk out of the store. It seemed her body temperature had risen ten degrees in the space of sixty seconds. She never considered the possibility of Joe moving on to someone else. Jealousy coursed through her veins at the thought of him with another woman.

You are betrothed to Aaron, she reminded herself.

Why didn't the thought bring the comfort she desired?

"They make a nice couple, don't you think?" Harv's voice from behind caused Anna to jump.

Anna placed a hand over her heart in an attempt to still its beat. "Harv, what are you doing here? I've never seen you in the shop before."

"Thought I'd check it out. Unless, of course, you don't want me in here."

Anna's heart lurched. "Why would you think that, Harv?" Anna asked the question, but she already knew the answer. Because Anna hadn't spoken to Harv or Joe, barring instances when they'd worked together and had to communicate, since they'd left her home.

"Seems to me you'd know the answer to that already. But I can clarify. You've changed, Miss Anna. The sweet woman who faithfully brought two lonely men lunch every day has been hiding somewhere. Either that or perhaps she doesn't want to associate with the likes of two certain vagabonds. I wonder if she's ashamed of us now." Harvey's honest eyes displayed his disappointment. "It's not the lunches that we miss, though. The lunches were mighty good, mind you. But it's that perty little angel with the sweet smile that brought 'em every day. That's what we've been missing. Have you seen her anywhere?"

Tears filled Anna's eyes. Harvey was right. The kindness she'd shown toward them – and the love – had been conditional. Selfish even. The moment she found out something negative, that there was nothing in it for her, she'd turned her back on both of them. She'd sent them back out into the cold. It shamed her to think of what a poor example of Christ's love she'd been.

"I'm sorry, Harv," Anna said as tears spilled onto her cheeks.

Harvey motioned toward the door where Aaron just walked in. "I'll go now," he dismissed himself to the back room.

Anna turned and quickly brushed her tears away before turning to greet Aaron.

Aaron raised his eyebrows and smiled. "Ready to go?"

"I need to stay here until Joe gets back. He took an early lunch," she explained.

Aaron frowned. "Right. Joe." He nodded. "When will he be back?"

"About forty-five minutes."

"Didn't he know that you usually take lunch at twelve?" he asked incredulously.

"It's okay, Aaron. I wanted –"

"No, it's not okay. He deliberately left early because he knew I would be taking you out." Aaron's frustration was quite evident. "Does he not have any respect for other peoples' time? Linda needs to fire him."

"What? No. That's not necessary."

"Where's your boss? I want to speak with her," he demanded.

Anna placed her hand over his in an attempt to calm him. "Aaron, leave it alone. Please." She reached up and turned his face toward hers.

Aaron released a slow breath when she caught his gaze. He nodded in compliance.

"Why don't you join us for dinner tonight instead?" Anna presented her peace offering. "I have some snacks in the fridge. I'll just eat my lunch in the break room today, okay?"

Reluctantly, Aaron agreed. He pecked her cheek, then grumbled when customers walked in the door. "I guess I better let you work. I'll see you tonight."

Anna moaned as she watched Aaron walk out the door, but quickly pasted on a happy face for the approaching customers.

After saying a quick hello to Linda, Joseph walked into the break room to don the apron she liked the workers to wear. Whistling, he walked to the peg that held the apron, quite aware that Anna sat at the small table eating her lunch.

Harv walked in from the back room. "How was your lunch date?"

Joe's eyes briefly moved to Anna's and quickly back to Harv's. He cleared his throat. "Uh…it was fine."

"That sure was one perty woman ya had there," Harv commented.

Joseph knew he was speaking this way to provoke Anna to jealousy, but he didn't appreciate it. "*Jah*, uh. We can talk about it later." Joe nodded toward Anna, his way of kindly telling Harvey to shut up.

The chair legs screeched across the floor as Anna moved to get up.

"Anna, you don't have to leave," Joe said, sending a disapproving look to Harvey.

Harvey finally got the message and went back to the storage room to give them privacy.

"No, it's okay." Anna continued to rise from her chair and moved to put the remainder of her food into the refrigerator.

"Please, Anna. Let's talk," Joe implored.

Anna worriedly glanced down at his hand on her arm. "I don't think that's a *gut* idea. I'm betrothed to Aaron now," she reminded him.

"About the quilts that were in my room –"

"Joe, please." Anna shook her head and briskly exited the room.

"Ugh!" Joe kicked his foot against the wall in frustration, then sunk into the chair Anna had just evacuated. What he felt like doing is picking it up and throwing it against the wall. But he was certain Linda would not appreciate that.

TWENTY-TWO

*L*inda poured two mugs of steaming coffee, then slid one across the table to Joe and took a seat. Harvey enjoyed sleeping in, so Joe never begrudged his old friend of the pleasure. Joseph suspected Linda knew what was coming before he ever uttered a word.

"I've decided to leave," Joe told his boss.

"Where will you go?" She took a small sip of her coffee.

Joseph looked into his mug, its contents already half gone. He'd always enjoyed coffee hot, the hotter the better. "I'm thinking of going to Paradise to visit my friend, Samuel Beachy."

"How long will you be gone?"

Joe shrugged. "I don't know. Maybe till February."

"But that's after Anna's…" She let her voice trail off, now sorry that she mentioned it. Of course, that's *why* he wouldn't return until February. It was after the wedding. "I'm sorry, Joe."

"Not as sorry as I am." Joe breathed deeply, attempting to keep his emotions in check.

"We'll miss you," Linda said. "I can't thank you enough for all you've done."

He shrugged. "It wasn't much."

"Yes, it was. It was a lot, Joe. Anna and her grandmother probably would have lost their home if it weren't for you."

"Linda, please. I'm trusting you not to saying anything to Anna."

"Yes, I know. But I have no idea why."

"I don't want her to feel obligated to me. If she knows…" His voice trailed off a moment while he gathered his thoughts. "I don't want her love based on something I did." Joe sighed. "Do you know how difficult it is to be accused – and convicted – of something you didn't do? Linda, this has been my entire life. I was shunned unjustly from my family and the only community I've ever known. I lost my friends and a very good, well-paying job because of something I did not do – and I went to prison for it. I wasn't there long, but the fact remains. And now, because of being accused of something once again, I've lost the love of my life. But I don't want her to love me for what I do or don't do. I want her to love me for who I am. Does that make sense?"

"It makes perfect sense."

"Life is so frustrating at times." He covered his face with his hands. "I'm sorry for dumping all this on you."

"That's okay, Joe. Everybody needs someone to talk to once in a while." Linda took another sip of coffee. "Have you given your cares to God?"

"No, thank you. I've tried all that. It doesn't work."

"Work? What do you mean?"

"Every time I start trusting God, something bad happens. All these things, they happened when I was trusting God."

"So, you don't trust God because bad things happen?" She raised a brow. "You don't want people to accuse you, but it seems you are accusing God. Did God shun you? Did God accuse you of wrong doing and put you into prison? Did God cause you to lose Anna? God has not done these things. Man has.

"I'll tell you what God did do. He sent Jesus to die on the cross so you could be saved. To forgive *your* sins. That doesn't sound like condemnation; that sounds like hope."

Joe sat silent, pondering her words.

"You don't want Anna to love for what you do but because of who you are, right? But you won't love God for who He is. And it seems like *you* may be falsely accusing Him of things He hasn't done," Linda said. "God doesn't promise us an easy life, Joe. But He does promise to love us and never leave us, no matter what happens."

"You sound like Harvey," he said wryly.

Linda smiled. "I knew there was a reason I liked him."

Joseph steadied himself as the buggy hit a large pothole and resumed his musings. He glanced at Jacob, eyeing his friend with admiration. What would it be like to be settled down and married to a woman you were crazy about? How different would life be if he had three sweet little girls like Jacob had? He'd watched how the girls would practically leap into his arms the moment he walked into the house. He'd seen how his wife's whole countenance brightened the moment their eyes met. His friend lived a life he could only dream about.

For Joseph, though, that dream seemed unattainable. Impossible, even.

"You look like you're a million miles away," Jacob commented.

Joe shook his head. "You know, Jacob, you're a lucky man."

"Well, I don't know how much luck has to do with it, but I am blessed." Jacob smiled. "What makes you say that?"

"It seems like you have it all. A wife, *kinner*, and probably your own home soon."

"God has been good for certain sure, but it hasn't all been easy." Jacob flicked the reins and veered the buggy a little to the right so a car could pass. "Rachel and I don't always see eye to eye." He chuckled, remembering their courting days. "She practically had to knock me out to get me to see that she loved me in the first place. I was pretty thick-headed.

"And my sister jumping the fence hadn't been easy either. We've dealt with some hardships. But *jah*, having Rachel by my side has made my burden a little lighter."

Joseph rubbed the back of his neck where his hair had grown out some. "I often wonder about my folks too. When I was put under the *Bann*, I imagine it was not easy for them."

"It seems your district was quite strict, *jah?*"

"One of the toughest, I hear." He shrugged.

"You'll be happy to know that Bishop Hostettler is pretty lenient – or maybe I should say merciful – for the most part. Not too many have been excommunicated in Paradise, or here, for that matter."

"*Jah*, I admit I was a little surprised how readily you accepted a shunned man. It would not be so in my old district. Seems like they were tolerant with certain things they should have been strict on, and strict on things they should have been tolerant on. Didn't make much sense in my mind." He shook his head.

"Rules can be good or bad. I don't think blatant sin should ever be tolerated. Especially if it's something *Der Herr* despises."

"Do you think he despises orange safety triangles?" Joseph chuckled, thinking how absurd it all sounded.

Jacob laughed. "Is that what you were shunned for?"

"No, but almost." He smiled. "I'm glad you invited me along today, I've been needing a breath of fresh air."

"I can use an extra set of eyes to help me pick out a *gut* mare. Rachel's been wanting to go riding." Jake smiled. "That's something we used to do all the time, but since the *kinner* have come we haven't had much opportunity."

Joseph imagined riding through an open field or into a copse of trees with Anna. "That sounds nice."

"Anything in particular you want to talk about?"

It seemed Jacob could read him well. Why did it seem certain friends could pick up on your moods? "*Jah*, I'm thinking of going to visit Samuel in Paradise."

"For how long?"

"Don't know. Might just stay there."

"Really? That's too bad. I was hoping you'd be staying around here. I don't really know too many folk in these parts. I was looking forward to having a friend close by." Jacob frowned. "Why are you leaving?"

"Simply put: Anna. I can't stay here and watch her marry someone else." Joe shook his head.

"I thought maybe there was something between the two of you when we first arrived. What happened?"

"Aaron brought up something from my past. Now she's convinced I'm some sort of crook."

Jacob lifted a brow. "Are you?"

Joseph shook his head in denial. "But it doesn't matter. She's supposed to marry him in February."

Jacob chuckled.

"Why are you laughing?" Here Joe was pouring his heart out and Jacob was laughing? He frowned in disapproval.

"I don't even think she likes Aaron. I don't see how she thinks she's going to marry him."

"What do you mean?"

"She's never in a good mood when he's around. And when he finally leaves the house, she sighs as though she's glad he's gone." Jacob cupped Joe's shoulder. "But when we first arrived, she seemed happy. You should have seen the way her face lit up when you walked in the room. You have something Aaron doesn't have."

"What's that?"

"Her heart. She obviously loves *you*."

TWENTY-THREE

*A*nna, *Mammi*, and Rachel all sat in the *schtupp* near the fire place with hot tea in hands. Anna glanced up at the clock again. It seemed like Jacob should have been back by now. They'd already finished supper, but set aside two plates for Jacob and Joe, knowing they'd be hungry upon their return.

The thought of Joseph being in the house again both excited and unnerved Anna. Perhaps when he arrived she should just go upstairs to her room. It would probably be best if she didn't see him. But something inside of her wanted to – longed to, even. Oh, what a jumble of emotions she was!

He's a thief, she reminded herself.

As the clip-clop of horses' hooves entered the driveway, Anna watched Rachel rush to the window. "They're here," her excited voice announced. She hurried to the door to gander at the new horse Jacob rode. Anna figured Joe must have driven the buggy home.

"It's a paint!" Rachel exclaimed. "I can't wait to ride her."

Anna smiled. Watching Rachel's reaction to the horse was like watching a child open up Christmas gift.

Several moments later, the sound of stomping boots on the back porch reached their ears. In spite of herself, Anna glanced up at Joe as they walked through the door. He was now wearing a black felt hat – an Amish hat. Anna thought he looked quite handsome, she had to admit. For a brief moment, their eyes locked until Joseph looked away.

"Your hat," she blurted out.

Joe offered a brief soft smile. "Picked it up in town." He removed his hat and placed it on the peg near the door.

Jacob spoke now, "He wanted to pick up a nice hat before he leaves for Paradise." Her cousin's gaze met hers, sensing her unspoken question. "Joe's leaving us."

Anna's heart clenched. "He is?" She looked to Joseph.

Joe nodded.

"When?" Her spoken words were almost a whisper.

"Tomorrow," Joe said quietly.

Mammi moved around them and sat two plates on the table for the men. She beckoned them to sit down. Rachel refilled the ladies' tea cups and they joined the men at the table.

Rachel spoke up, "Speaking of Paradise, Leah called."

"My *Mamm*?" Jacob asked. "What did she call about?"

Rachel's tone sobered. "It's not good news, Jacob."

"What? What is it? What's wrong?" Anna sensed panic in Jacob's voice.

"Samuel was in a buggy accident," Rachel said.

Jacob locked eyes with Joseph. "Samuel? Samuel Beachy?"

Joe's head lowered.

"He died, Jacob," Rachel finally divulged.

Joe spoke now, a look of unbelief flashed across his face. "Samuel Beachy is dead?"

"That is what Jacob's mother said," *Mammi* volunteered. "Apparently, there was a woman with him too. She has been hospitalized."

"His wife?" Joseph asked.

"No, Samuel was a widower," Jacob said. "His wife died of cancer not that long ago."

The news of Samuel's sudden death had been shocking and saddening. He'd had no idea that his friend had been married, nor that he was a widower. Joseph chided himself for not visiting sooner. Now he'd never have the opportunity to see Samuel again.

He couldn't help but feel like God was throwing him for another loop. What was he going to do now? That had been his escape, his excuse to leave. With Samuel now gone, he had no good excuse.

"I'd like to go to the funeral." Jacob looked to his wife.

Rachel nodded, but Joseph sensed a bit of anxiousness.

Jake seemed to read his wife's thoughts. "You and the girls may stay here, Rachel." He turned to Joe. "You want to come to the funeral with me?"

Joseph nodded. "I'd like that. When is it?"

"In two days," Rachel informed them.

"We'll have to leave tomorrow," Jacob said.

"Already?" Joe turned to Anna, surprised that she'd spoken. "Uh…I mean, does this mean that you won't be working at the store? We've been busy lately," she recovered.

"I'm certain you and Linda can handle it, *jah*?" Joe answered. He finished the remainder of his supper, then looked to Jacob. "What time do you want to leave?"

"I was thinking mid-morning would be a *gut* time. Say eight o'clock?"

"Sounds *gut*. Well, I better be going. It's getting late." Joseph turned to *Mammi*. "Thank you for the fine supper."

Anna watched in dismay as Joseph lifted his hat from the rack, placed it on his head, and stepped outside into the night.

Anna placed a bolt of fabric back on the shelf after cutting four yards for a customer. She ambled over to the cash register and rung up the sale, glad when the customer finally exited the store.

This was not a good day. In fact, it had been terrible.

Everything she'd done had turned out wrong. The four yards of material she'd just cut was supposed to be three. She'd inadvertently spoken *Deitsh* to a group of women who stared back at her as though she were an alien from outer space. She'd accidentally given a customer back a one dollar bill instead of a ten and the customer complained to her boss that Anna had been trying to cheat her.

And it was only ten-thirty.

She hadn't slept well at all last night. The thought of Joseph leaving for good didn't settle well. When she finally did fall asleep, she'd dreamt about him. Why couldn't she get him out of her mind? Every time she reminded herself that Joseph Bender was a thief, her heart rebelled. Understanding her chaotic emotions seemed impossible.

By the time she arrived at the store this morning, Joe had already been gone. Gone, that's it. No *nice knowing ya*, no *maybe we'll see each other again sometime*, no anything.

He hadn't even said *goodbye*.

TWENTY-FOUR

*J*oseph closed his eyes as he pondered the task ahead of him: attending Samuel Beachy's funeral. Why is it that life presented so many challenges? And regrets. If he wouldn't have hesitated when he first considered going to see Samuel, he'd have had a chance to see his friend alive.

He hadn't known Samuel all that well, but during the summer Samuel had gone to Ohio to work with his uncle Timothy, they had bonded. Samuel was helping with the harvest and Joseph had been filling in for his brother at the buggy shop. Samuel was a buggy maker by trade, so naturally he asked a lot of questions about the different styles of buggies in the neighboring districts.

They were both in *rumspringa* at the time, and although it was *verboten* in Joseph's district, a lot of young men rebelled anyway. One of Joseph's friends owned a car, so they'd go to the *Englischers'* movie theater, roller skating rink, and bowling alley. Joseph had been courting Mary at the time, so he was willing to do whatever it took to keep her away from home. Samuel had met a girl from his uncle's district named Carolanne. Jacob had just recently informed Joseph that Carolanne eventually became Samuel's wife.

Joseph hadn't seen Samuel since that summer and often wondered what became of him. If he'd known Samuel had moved back to Ohio, he might have gone to see him after his shunning. It was a dark time in his life and he'd been desperate for friends. Not only was he dealing with his excommunication, but he'd also been mourning Mary's recent death.

Apparently, Samuel had only moved back to Paradise a few weeks ago. After his wife Carolanne passed on, he decided to move back home to be near his family and close friends.

"We're almost there," Jacob informed Joe.

Joseph opened his eyes and looked around. This is what he loved about the Amish culture – uniformity. He could visit nearly any Amish district and feel a sense of home and commonality, a comfort unknown in the *Englisch* world he'd lived. For the most part, a lot of districts were the same by appearance. The houses and barns were similar, the dress was always decent and modest, transportation was by horse and buggy – although he'd heard that there were some faster Amish groups that even drove automobiles and used electric. In his former Swartzentruber sect, they weren't even allowed to ride in a vehicle unless it was an emergency.

One thing he greatly favored about the faster Amish groups was indoor plumbing. Using an outhouse still didn't bother him, but indoor facilities were so much more pleasant. Jacob had informed him that his maternal grandmother ran a bed 'n breakfast and that was where they'd be staying. He said the bed 'n breakfast contained three indoor restrooms. Imagine that - three restrooms in one Amish home!

"See that stand? That's been there forever. My *Mamm* said she used work out there selling stuff," Jacob mentioned, pointing out an old road-side produce stand. "This is the turn to my *Grossdawdi*'s place."

Joseph surveyed the property, still colorful from the vestiges of fall. "They haven't had snow yet?"

"Apparently not." The air was cool, but not like the normal chill this time of year. "The weather had still been nice when Rachel and I left. I never expected to be back so soon."

Joseph eyed a large, white, octagonal, wooden structure. "That's a nice gazebo."

"I helped *Grossdawdi* paint that a few years ago. I'm surprised it's still standing. *Mamm* said she and *Dat* shared their first kiss in that gazebo," Jake volunteered.

"This looks like a nice place." He examined the beautiful large home with its exquisite wraparound porch. "Where will the funeral be?"

"At Samuel's folks' place. And of course we'll go out to the cemetery," Jacob said. "But for now, let's go inside and enjoy some of my *grossmudder's* delicious cooking."

"Sounds good to me!" Joe agreed.

The viewing at the home of Samuel's parents had been interesting. Not being from Paradise, Joseph felt slightly out of place, even though the People had been kind and hospitable. Joe had the opportunity to meet Samuel's folks as well his brother Peter and his sister-in-law Deborah. Deborah and Peter had a little boy that looked a lot like Samuel, everyone had thought, including Joseph.

Jacob had also introduced him to the church leaders, primarily Bishop Hostetler, who served as the bishop in Anna's district as well. He had heard many good things about Bishop Hostettler which somewhat surprised him. He had the notion that all bishops were unyielding and stern like Bishop Burkholder had been. But one look at Bishop Hostettler's countenance told Joe there was something different about him. He was unsure whether he equated the look to kindness or mischief, perhaps a bit of both.

If Joseph had the opportunity, he planned to speak with the bishop regarding his standing in the church. He admitted to being nervous about it, knowing he'd been shunned and all. But he hoped Bishop Hostettler would give him the benefit of the doubt. Whether he found someone to marry or not, Joe decided he wouldn't mind conforming to the ways of the People here.

After he and Jacob sat through the preaching service, Jacob took him on a tour of Paradise, showing him everything he'd loved about the community. They drove by Philip King's herb shop where Jacob and his family had purchased most of the medicines they used growing up, and he shared a story of how *Mamm*'s *Englisch* friend had been bitten by a snake one time.

He took Joe by Miller's Pond where he'd said he spent many winters ice skating and had swam in the summer time. He'd also said he'd been baptized there. Joseph thought it fascinating because all the Amish districts he'd ever heard of had just poured the water over the head – that's how he'd been baptized. But Jacob told him that was not the way of the Bible; something he'd have to look into later if he wanted to become part of a New Order.

Lastly, Jacob had taken him to Miller's Bridge. It was mostly a private covered bridge that the *Englischers* didn't know about. The beautiful bridge was constructed mostly of wood and looked to be well over a hundred years old, judging by the lumber used. Joseph stared up at the magnificent structure and read hundreds of initials, sweethearts that had probably once had special moments under the cover of this 'kissing bridge'.

Jacob beckoned him over to one of the wooden beams. "Read that." He smiled.

Joseph surveyed the carved heart with initials inside. "J plus R. Jacob and Rachel?" He raised an eyebrow and grinned.

Jake nodded.

"How many of these people do you think got married?"

"Let's see…there's J and S, that's Jonathan and Susie. He's the minister of this district. J and L." He laughed. "That's Bishop Hostettler and his wife Lydia."

"No way, really?" Joseph shook his head in disbelief. "The bishop carved initials into a bridge? Wow, he really *is* different. If I were to have done something like that back home, I'd probably have gotten a *gut* whipping."

"Well, he hasn't always been bishop. I suspect he did that when they were courtin'." Jacob rubbed his chin. "I guess that's why he's such a good bishop. He knows he's human and that others are too. He's genuine and understanding. I reckon that's part of the reason why I didn't balk at moving to Anna's district."

"Do you have a knife?"

Jacob nodded and handed Joe his pocket knife.

Joseph found an uncarved area and engraved J plus A.

Jacob raised his eyebrows. "Are you going to make that a reality?"

One side of Joe's mouth tipped up. "I hope so."

TWENTY-FIVE

A swirl of steam from Joseph's coffee rose from his mug as he sipped the beverage, sitting in a hickory rocker in Bishop Judah Hostettler's home. Or rather his son Joshua's home. Bishop Hostettler and his wife occupied the one of the small *dawdi hauser* connected to the large main house. Joshua's aged in-laws occupied the other small *dawdi haus.*

Joseph briefly wondered what it would have been like to grow up in a district such as this. They still valued the same things: God, family, and community, but there was an element of grace that had been missing from his former district. The People here seemed happier, freer. Yet at the same time, they had a set of rules and traditions, or perhaps a common bond of faith, woven together by love.

"So, you were raised Amish, you say?" Judah Hostettler asked.

"Swartzentruber." Joe nodded.

"I see."

Joseph swallowed hard. He admitted to himself that he was nervous, although he'd been assured he didn't need to be. "I have been excommunicated."

Judah nodded. "I see."

"Uh...I wouldn't repent." Joe clarified, slowly finding his voice. "They had a lot of rules – unnecessary rules, I'd thought. But I was shunned because I went to the *Englisch* authorities on a matter."

Judah's eyebrows lifted. "What was this matter?"

"My *aldi*. Her brother was a very depraved man. He did things to her that he shouldn't have. I went to the elders and they put a restriction on him, but other than that, nothing was done. This man was wicked and he needed to be dealt with." A bead of sweat formed on his brow as he explained the situation. "I didn't want to see Mary violated. No person should have to live in fear in their own home. In the place that's supposed to be a safe haven. I figured going to the *Englisch* was better than me killing him – which is probably what would have happened eventually." Heat rose in his veins as he remembered Mary's wicked brother.

"This man, the brother, he went to jail?"

"No. Mary ended up dying in an accident before she could testify. The case was dismissed. They said they could not prosecute without a witness. As far as I know, he still lives in Bishop Burkholder's district."

A scowl crossed the bishop's face. It seemed as though he shared Joseph's thoughts. "You did the right thing, son."

"I did?" He'd always thought it was the right thing. What else could he have done – turn a blind eye like everyone else? But hearing a bishop say the words gave Joseph's actions validation.

"I believe I would have done the same thing."

Joe released a contented breath. "So, if I decide to join this district, I will have a good standing?" Joseph's hopeful expression caused the Judah to smile.

"Most definitely." Judah's countenance then sobered. "Of course, there are certain tenets that you must adhere to. I will have my minister, Jonathan, give you a copy of our creed. Our *Ordnung*. If you agree to it, then we will proceed with your membership."

"Will my membership be transferable?"

"Were you wanting to join here or in one of the other districts I oversee?"

"I'm unsure yet."

"I see. Your membership will be transferable to any of the districts I oversee. Our doctrine is one and the same."

Joseph agreed, ready to take the next step in becoming a member.

"You are awesome!"

Joseph stared at Minister Fisher with his mouth agape. He'd never heard any Amish leader speak this way before. "I am?"

"You'd better believe it. Do you know how many people have the courage to stand up and do the right thing? Not very many. Most folks are concerned with themselves and how it will affect them. But you – you stood up for what was right even though you knew you would probably be facing the *Bann*." Jonathan held out his hand for Joe to shake. "You left everything for the sake of the truth and right."

"*Jah*, I guess I did."

"Maybe you'll be the next bishop of this district. Of course, God's the one that does the choosing. But after Judah leaves us, which I hope is a long way off. I love that man – he's my father-in-law, you know – just don't tell him I said that, the love part. He'll give me a hard time for sure and for certain." Jonathan grinned.

"Okay, I won't." Joe still experienced a bit of nervousness, although Jonathan was easygoing.

"Now, Judah sent you to me because you want to become part of the flock. Am I correct?"

"*Jah*."

Minister Fisher seemed to compose his relaxed demeanor some. "First things first. If you were to die right now, are you certain sure you'd go to Heaven?"

This question certainly wasn't what Joe was expecting. But, then again, *nothing* in this district had been as he'd suspected. And he found himself liking it. He thought on Jonathan's question. "I can't say I am sure. I mean, I *hope* that I'll get into

Heaven. Besides being shunned and falsely accused for things I didn't do, I don't think I've been too bad."

"So, you believe you've been pretty good?"

Joseph nodded.

"Just a minute."

Joseph watched in confusion as Jonathan walked out of the room. He returned shortly with an old, dirty tooth brush in his hand. He held the toothbrush out to Joe. "Here, go brush your teeth with this."

Joseph's mouth hung open. "What?"

"Brush your teeth."

Joe shook his head, thinking Minister Fisher must be *ab im kopp.* "I don't think so."

"Why not?"

"Because. That toothbrush is disgusting. I wouldn't want to stick that dirty thing in my mouth." Joseph cringed at the deplorable thought.

"Why is it that you, being a mere man, will not accept a dirty toothbrush, but you expect a holy and perfect God to accept your filthy rags?"

"I'm not sure I understand what you mean."

Jonathan nodded. He reached for a Bible on the end table next to his chair, then opened it up. *"But we are all as an unclean thing, and all our righteousnesses are as filthy rags..."* He turned to another place. *"There is none righteous, no, not one."* He set the Bible down. "When you offer your good works – or righteousness – to God, He sees it as a filthy rag."

"He does?"

"Yep." He opened his Bible again. "Look at this. *Not by works of righteousness which we have done, but according to his mercy he saved us...*" Jonathan flipped to another passage. "*For by grace are ye saved though faith; and that not of yourselves: it is the gift of God: Not of works, lest any man should boast.*"

Joseph scratched his head as the truths Jonathan was sharing dawned on him. "So, if I get to Heaven by being good – which is impossible – then I would have something to boast about."

Jonathan clapped his hands together. "That's right. God doesn't want us bragging about ourselves, He alone deserves glory. But even more shocking is this verse here: *I do not frustrate the grace of God: for if righteousness come by the law, then Christ is dead in vain.* You see, if we could simply get to Heaven by being good enough, then Jesus Christ would have died for nothing. And trying to get to Heaven by our own works is an insult to God. I say that because He has offered us a free gift: full payment for our sins through the blood of Jesus. Bringing our filthy rags to God as payment for our sins is rejecting God's perfect sacrifice."

"Oh, wow! I never thought of it that way. That means that Jesus is the only way to Heaven."

"Bull's eye. *Jesus saith unto him, I am the way, the truth, and the life: no man cometh unto the Father, but by me,*" he quoted John fourteen verse six.

Joseph laughed. "I think you can put your dirty toothbrush away now. I won't be needing it."

"Good, I hoped not. I hate looking at that thing. It's gross."

TWENTY-SIX

*J*oseph felt like a new man. It seemed as though God had taken his burdens and replaced them with wings. He finally felt like he had direction in his life, a definite vision.

No, the goal was not Anna. But he hoped that somehow Anna would come to love and respect him as she once had. In a way, she'd inadvertently opened his eyes to the vision. But there had been several catalysts along the path to his discovery. Anna had been just one, Harv had been another, Linda's confidence in him propelled the dream further, and now he knew his journey to Paradise had been a Divine appointment.

Jonathan's words of commendation had set him on a new path. And after he'd experienced his secret encounter with *Der Herr*, he had been given strength and hope. Now he planned to use it for God's glory.

He thought back on his past. There was something Mary had said that he never understood until now. He vividly remembered the conversation, as though it had just taken place yesterday:

It was the night of Mary's death. Her eyes had been sparkling, like he'd never seen them before. He knew it was more than just the pleasure she derived from being in his presence. It was something else. "Joseph, I want to tell you about something."

Joseph had been driving the buggy and they were approaching a bend in the road. He briefly glanced at her and smiled, granting permission to continue speaking. He'd been holding her hand, but now held the reins steady with both hands, keeping to the side so vehicles could pass.

"I had a secret encounter."

The mysterious words piqued his interest. "A secret encounter?"

She reached into her purse and pulled out a small *Englisch* Bible – something *verboten* in their Swartzentruber district. "You mustn't tell anyone."

His eyes widened.

She held the small book to her chest, as though it had been the most precious thing in the world. "A secret encounter with Jesus."

It was then the bright lights had flashed in his face, followed by a screeching sound, and subsequent crash. That's all he remembered prior to waking up in the hospital and learning of Mary's death. After that, nothing else mattered.

He'd completely forgotten the conversation, as though his mind had blocked it out. But now he knew. He knew in his spirit exactly what Mary's secret encounter had been: she'd accepted Christ as her Saviour! What a wonderful *gut* revelation.

As Joseph looked into the medicine cabinet's mirror, he carefully shaved the excess hair from his face. He pondered how he might tell Anna about all that had happened in Paradise, as he prepared for work this morning. Linda had been relieved when he'd called late last night and told her he was back. Apparently, the Christmas shopping frenzy had not let up in his absence.

Harvey was happy to have him back. And Joe had to admit that he'd missed his old buddy. Harvey had said he noticed a difference in Joe, although they'd only spoken for an hour prior to turning in for the night. Harvey had been thrilled to hear Joseph's confession.

Joe now moved throughout the shop, turning on the lights. He'd leave the door locked until Linda or Anna arrived. Surveying the store, he took a mental inventory of the things that had sold. One of *Mammi's* quilts was gone. Joseph's face brightened when he saw another quilt had replaced it. Anna and *Mammi* would be doing just fine financially for a while. The thought gave him a sense of satisfaction.

He glanced up at the clock. Linda would probably be coming soon, so he moved to the break room to start a pot of coffee. With that done, he sat behind the counter and took out his Bible. Daily reading had not been a habit, so it didn't come naturally to him. However, when he picked up God's Word and began reading, sometimes he had trouble setting it back down. The truths he'd unearthed in his brief moments of study had been amazing. Every time he read something new, he was blown away. There were so many treasures within the pages of this amazing book.

A knock on the door caused him to look up from his reading. It was Anna. What was she doing here this early? She usually didn't show up until after Linda. He rushed to the door to unlock it, not wanting her to have to wait long in the cold. When Joe reached the door, he noticed Aaron behind her. He couldn't help the groan that escaped his lips. He turned the key and allowed them entrance.

Anna's eyes lit up as though she'd just realized it was him. "Joe?"

He was speechless when Anna threw her arms around him. He hugged her back, then let go when he noticed Aaron's scowl.

"You're back! I thought you were gone for good," she said.

"No. I just went to Paradise for Samuel's funeral."

Aaron was visibly becoming impatient.

Bless them that curse you. Joe looked to Anna and Aaron. "Hey, I just made some coffee. Would you like a cup?"

"*You* made coffee?" Aaron scoffed.

"Sure. I'd love some," Anna said. She turned to Aaron. "Do you need to go?"

Aaron nodded, eyeing Joseph warily. He leaned over and kissed Anna's cheek. "I'll see you tonight when I pick you up."

Anna smiled and escorted him to the door. She turned the key to lock the door after Aaron exited. They wouldn't officially open till eight o'clock.

Joe smiled when Anna entered the break room. He handed her a cup of steaming coffee. "Do you need the cream and sugar?"

"I can get it." Anna moved to the refrigerator to get the creamer. She poured some into her mug, added a spoon of sugar, and then sat down across the table from Joseph.

"How are the wedding plans coming along?" Joe attempted to make small talk.

Anna frowned. "I'd rather not talk about that."

Joe shrugged. "Okay. What do you want to talk about?"

"I had thought that you left for good. Jacob said you were leaving us." Tears rose in her eyes, something Joe didn't expect. "I thought you'd left without saying goodbye."

"Did it matter?"

Anna stared at him forlornly. "Of course, it mattered. I thought I might never see you again."

"I don't understand."

"Just because we aren't together anymore, doesn't mean that I hate you. It doesn't mean that I don't care for you."

"What does that mean?"

She clasped her hands together. "We can still be friends, can't we?"

"Aren't you afraid I'm going to steal something from your purse? I'm a thief, you know," he said sardonically.

"Can we put that behind us?"

He raised a cynical brow and crossed his arms. "I don't know. Can we?"

Anna wanted to scream. Where was the easy talk and mutual admiration they'd once shared? When she thought he'd left for good, her mind had filled with a thousand things she would say to him if she ever got a chance to speak with him again. Things like: *I'm sorry. I was wrong to treat you that way. I missed you.*

But it seemed things were different now. Her mistrust in him had erected an invisible wall – one that must be torn down before they could ever have any kind of relationship. Relationships were built on trust. But how could she trust a known thief?

That was one question she hadn't figured out.

Aaron couldn't believe Joseph Bender had come back. He thought he'd been rid of him for good when Anna said that he'd gone. Now he was back, probably trying to wiggle his way back into Anna's heart at this very moment. He had to do something. He swiftly moved to the phone in his shop and searched through the telephone book. He found the number he was looking for and placed a quick call.

TWENTY-SEVEN

Today hadn't gone the way Joe had planned. It seemed the wedge between him and Anna had been driven further, forcing them apart even more. When Anna had entered the shop this morning, hope had filled his heart. But the scenario he had imagined never happened. How could they get back to that place where they once communed together?

Anna hadn't been in a good mood today. After their brief conversation in the break room this morning, they hadn't spoken two words to each other.

A man walked in the door carting a large bouquet of flowers. Were they from Linda's husband? Joseph smiled.

"Is there an Anna Smucker here?" the man from the florist asked.

Joe's smile turned upside down. He pointed to where Anna helped a customer.

Joe watched as Anna's face lit up in delight. She read the small card attached to the flowers and smiled. When she unintentionally caught Joe's eye, she abruptly turned around. He watched as she excused herself, then cheerfully took the flowers to the break room.

Joseph double checked the door to be certain Anna was still assisting a customer. He quickly and quietly tip-toed over to the bouquet of flowers, searching for the card.

"What are you doing?"

Joseph jumped. "Harvey, you scared me to death."

Harvey chuckled. "Caught ya with your hand in the cookie jar, did I?"

"Shh…just keep watch while I read the card." He held the small envelope in his hand.

"You know, you really shouldn't be doing that."

"You're right." Joe moved to put the card back.

Harv began his exposition from memory, *"To my beloved Anna, You are the most wonderful woman in the world. Flowers are lovely, but they pale in comparison to your beauty. Looking forward to tonight. Yours alone, Aaron."* Harvey's face brightened. "Pretty debonair fellow, wouldn't you say?"

"Is that really what it says?" Joe lifted a brow.

Harv nodded sheepishly. "I read it earlier. Figured you'd be wantin' to know what it said."

Joe plopped down into one of the chairs at the table and stared miserably at the beautiful red roses. "What am I going to do, Harv?"

"Why don't you pray? Then wait on the Lord."

"Should I just stand by and watch Anna marry Aaron?"

"Pray. And wait on the Lord."

Joseph sucked in a deep breath and released it heavily. "Okay."

Aaron walked into Threads of Beauty ten minutes prior to closing time. Anna was glad to see him, anxious to be on her way home. The atmosphere had been way too tense in the store today. She thought she'd be thrilled to see Joe again, and she had been this morning. But it seemed there had been a brick wall between them since.

"I need to wait until Linda arrives before I can leave," she informed Aaron. "She had some errands to run." Anna refolded several scraps of material on the Clearance table and organized them as they'd been earlier in the day. Why is it that customers could never replace items the way they found them? Oh well, just part of the job. At least it kept her busy.

Aaron nodded and took a seat and pulled out a newspaper from his coat. He glanced over at Joe behind the cash register, still irked by his presence.

Linda entered the store carrying several bolts of fabric and Joe rushed to help her. They took her purchases into the back room, then Linda beckoned Anna to the back room as well.

Aaron eyed the cash register, a dozen thoughts swirling

in his mind. *It's now or never*, he told himself. He rushed to the register and quickly opened it. Aaron lifted the drawer and grabbed the large bills from underneath. He rapidly closed the drawer and glanced around for a place to stash the money. He spied Joe's Bible on one of the inside shelves. *Perfect!*

Anna and Linda walked out of the break room. Anna smiled at Aaron as he patiently sat where she'd last seen him, still reading his newspaper. "I'll be ready to go in just a few minutes, Aaron. Linda and I need to go over today's sales receipts and count the money. You don't mind waiting, do you?"

"No, of course not, *Schatzi*." Aaron's eyes sparkled.

Anna opened up the cash register and removed the drawer. She gasped when she didn't see the large bills underneath.

Linda moved close and whispered, "Anna, is there a problem?"

Anna gestured to the empty drawer bottom. "The money's gone...you don't think..." She hated to think the worst of Joe, but history spoke for itself.

"Well, perhaps there's another explanation. Maybe it's around here somewhere."

Anna look at the shelf beneath the counter. Something green peeked out from Joseph's Bible. She pointed it out to Linda.

Linda frowned. "Oh no." She sighed.

Aaron walked up. "Is there a problem?"

"There's money missing," Anna volunteered.

"I'll call the police," Aaron said, hastily making his way out the door.

Joseph stood in shock as the officer brought his hands behind his back and placed the cuffs on his wrists. Another officer stood stalwart, reading him his rights. He kept silent.

Anna's disappointed gaze darted elsewhere when he forlornly looked her way, but not before he recognized the shame. It was the same look his father had given him before he'd walked out the door the last time.

Pray and wait on the Lord.

This time, no matter what happened, he couldn't let his faith waver. But it was different now. Somehow, he felt peace instead of fear.

God was in control.

TWENTY-EIGHT

Anna wrapped herself in one of *Mammi's* quilts and slipped outside into the cold night. She sunk down into the hickory rocker on their small front porch. The sky was clear and the air crisp. It seemed she could see every star visible to the naked eye. Each one sparkled with a majesty all their own, manifesting their Creator's magnificent glory.

A tear slipped down Anna's cheek.

Recounting the things she'd seen and read to the police had been so difficult. And then when the officers slapped the handcuffs on Joseph. It had been terrible. She felt like she was betraying a friend. And, in essence, she was.

As she'd watched the officers walk out with Joe, then put him into their patrol car, it was all she could do to not break down in tears. As the patrol car drove away, she felt a piece of her heart leave too. It had been the most miserable thing she'd ever experienced.

So many times she'd reminded herself that Joseph Bender was a thief. But every time the words formed in her mind, she'd prayed that somehow they weren't true. But they were.

What now?

She wished *Mamm* or *Dat* were here to talk to. It was times like this she missed her parents most. What would they have said at a time like this? When she'd been younger, she'd never thought she might have to face life – and marriage – without them. She'd always taken for granted that they'd be there for her. Never had their absence, and the consequent void, been so evident, as it was now.

Anna turned when she heard the door creak open.

Rachel walked out carrying two mugs of hot cocoa. She handed one to Anna.

"You couldn't sleep either?" Anna offered a faint smile.

"It's been crazy, *jah?*"

"*Jah.*"

"Jacob thinks that Joseph is innocent," Rachel blurted out.

Anna raised a brow. "He does?"

"He said they had some good conversations when they traveled to Paradise for Samuel's funeral. He asked Joseph point blank if he was a thief, and he said no. So either he's innocent, or he's a thief *and* a liar."

Anna chuckled wryly. "And the reason I liked him in the first place is because I'd thought he was honest."

"May I offer some advice?"

Anna nodded.

"Just give it to God. He'll work it all out in His own way and in His own time," Rachel encouraged. "This is a burden you don't need to carry. *Casting all your care upon him; for he careth for you*," she quoted.

"Thank you. I think I will."

Rachel stood up from the rocker beside Anna. "Anna, anytime you need to talk, I'm here. And I don't know if Jacob told you, but we found a place. It's just down the road, three farms away."

"Really? That's wonderful." Anna's face brightened. "When will you and Jacob be moving?"

"Hopefully, by February. So you'll have to put up with us a bit longer."

"Oh no, we love having you here," Anna replied.

Rachel smiled before stepping into the house.

Anna bowed her head and whispered a silent prayer. In spite of all she'd been through, God was still good. He'd been her strength when her folks died. He'd been there through all the trials she'd gone through lately. And she knew He'd be there guiding her future. *Jesus Christ the same yesterday, and to day, and for ever.* It was that steady Rock that kept her going, and that kept her strong.

Anna stood to go back into the house. Bright lights shined in the distance, most likely a passing car. She paused when she realized the vehicle had turned into their lane and was approaching rapidly. Who would be visiting this time of night?

She looked closer and recognized the car. It was Linda's.

"Anna!" Linda called from the car.

She watched as Linda, her husband, and Harv all exited the vehicle with haste.

"What's going on?" Anna stared wide-eyed.

Linda held up a laptop computer. "I need to show you something."

Anna led the way into the house, offering her guests a seat at the kitchen table. Rachel was already seated at the table with her Bible open in front of her. She rose and walked to the cook stove, placing a large pot on top. She opened the water reservoir and ladled out some hot water for cocoa and coffee.

"You better get your grandma and Jacob. They'll be wantin' to see this too!" Harv bellowed.

"Shh…the *kinner* are sleeping," Anna cautioned.

She returned a moment later with *Mammi* and Jacob. Rachel handed everyone a mug and brought out some instant coffee and cocoa mix. While the others prepared their drinks, Linda powered on her computer. When the screensaver appeared, she reached into her purse and pulled out a small plastic rectangular object.

"What is that?" Anna asked.

"It's an SD card. It can hold a lot of information," Linda informed her.

"And video!" Harv added.

"Just watch," Linda advised. She pressed a few keys on her laptop and a video began playing.

"That's the store!" Anna said, surprised.

Linda nodded. "Joe began installing a surveillance system for me before he went to Paradise for the funeral. He ran into some difficulties, so he wasn't able to finish it before he left. I didn't know this, but Harv had begun working on it and actually got it to work. Everything that happened in the store today is on this video."

Harvey pointed to the screen and Anna squinted to see the image. "That's Aaron," she said.

"Yep, that's Aaron all right," Harv agreed.

Anna's jaw dropped when she saw Aaron sneakily open the cash register and hide the money in Joseph's Bible. She stood speechless.

"Anna, there's more," Linda said. "Joe didn't want me to say anything, but I'm going to anyway. The Christmas bonus I gave you last week – it came from Joseph's paycheck."

Anna's eyes filled with tears.

"That's not all," Linda continued. She typed 'Threads of Beauty' into the search engine and a colorful page opened up. "Do those quilts look familiar?"

Mammi spoke up. "Those are my quilts – the ones that were hidden under the bed!"

"That's right," Linda said. "Joe volunteered to set up a website for the store. For free. He knew you'd been struggling financially and he wanted to see if he could help by promoting the store online. That's why we've been getting so much business lately. He took the quilts so he could take photographs and post them online."

Tears streamed down Anna's face and she sobbed into her hands. Harvey pulled her close and patted her back. Anna finally found her voice. "So he's been innocent this whole time?"

"That Aaron boy should be the one sitting in that jail cell right now. Not Joe," Harvey uttered with a scowl.

"Have you shown this to the police?" Jacob asked.

"No," Linda said. "I wanted Anna to see it first. But I plan to take it to them tonight."

"May I go with you?" Anna asked through her tears.

"Of course," Linda answered.

TWENTY-NINE

oseph sat on the small firm bed in his cell, his hands clasped together and head bent in prayer. A metal click drew his attention to the lock as a correctional officer opened the cell door. He stared at the officer wide eyed.

"Bail has been posted. You're free to go until your trial," the officer informed him.

Who posted bail for me? He wondered.

The officer walked him to the main booking office and they handed over his personal belongings. After he changed back into his street clothes, he was escorted to the outer waiting room.

Joe's mouth dropped open. "Bishop Hostettler?"

"I was already on my way to see you when I found out what happened," Judah said. "*Kumm*, I have somebody you might want to see. We hired a driver."

Confusion displayed on Joseph's face.

"I'm preaching this Sunday at the Girods' place," the bishop informed him. "Do you know them?"

"No. I haven't met them yet."

"I'll be staying in their *dawdi haus* over the weekend. You have been granted permission to stay too." Judah led the way out to the parking lot, where a van waited for them.

"I have?"

When they neared the van, an Amish couple stood beside it. Joseph examined them as he and the bishop came closer. He suddenly stopped in his tracks and stared in disbelief.

The woman rushed toward him, tears in her eyes. "Joseph?"

He gulped hard and his voice faltered. "*Mamm?*" His eyes wandered beyond where she stood. "*Dat?*"

"*Jah*, it is us, *Sohn*," his father replied.

Joseph couldn't take his eyes off of them. He stood in the cold, unaffected by the chill. "What are you doing here?"

The bishop spoke up, "Why don't we talk about this on the way to the Girods' place?"

Joseph, along with his parents, and Judah, all filed into the van. On the journey to their place of respite, Joseph's folks filled him in on all that had happened since he'd left. They apologized for their harsh treatment of him and informed him that they, too, had eventually left the Swartzentruber Amish. He learned that Mary's brother ended up going to prison after he was reported by someone else. His folks now lived in Southeastern Ohio, which was a lot closer to Bishop Hostettler's district, than the other sect up North.

"How did you know I was here?" He wondered aloud.

His father pointed to Judah. "The bishop called and spoke with your Uncle John a couple of weeks ago; he's still a minister up there. Judah asked about you and your standing in the church. John knew we were looking for you, so he contacted us right away."

Joseph searched Judah's face for more answers.

"Your Anna had contacted me a few weeks back. She asked about you being under *The Bann* and whether it was possible to lift it. So I did some investigating." Judah's eyes sparkled. "And, of course, after our conversation in Paradise and your meeting with Minister Fisher, I think we can safely say that the *Bann* has been lifted."

Joseph shook his head in amazement. He felt like crying. He felt like yelling out "THANK YOU" to God. But he didn't do either of those things. He simply bowed his head and whispered a humble prayer. God understood his heart.

God was so, so good!

Anna had been happy, and disappointed at the same time, to learn that Joseph had already been released. What bothered her most is that she now had no idea where he was. The jail would not release that information.

They'd gone to the store to see if he was in the room he shared with Harv, but he was not there. Where could he have gone? Worry lines formed on Anna's brow as she pictured him going back onto the streets. At her insistence, Linda drove around town in hopes of finding Joe. But it was for naught. He was nowhere to be found.

Regret clamped down on her heart once again. She should have known. She should have trusted Joe in the first place. She never should have allowed Aaron back into her life. How could she have been such a *dummkopp*?

Joseph's heart lifted as he sang songs of adoration to his Maker. Not only was this the first service he'd attended in many years, it was the first service he'd attended as a true child of God. This day would have been perfect if not for one thing.

His eyes meandered to the opposite side of the room where the women worshipped. Anna looked so depressed, it broke his heart. She scarcely allowed herself to lift her eyes to his. He understood what she must be feeling.

After the service, the bishop had introduced him and his folks to several people in the district. He determined to speak with Anna before she left for home today, and he set out to find her. He searched inside the barn and house, but didn't see her. Upon going outside, he found her walking by herself out in the cold.

"Anna!" he called to her.

She halted at the sound of his voice and briefly glanced his way, but continued in the same direction.

Joe had to run to catch up with her. "Anna, wait! Stop, please." By the time he caught up with her, he was nearly out of breath.

"What?"

Joseph was tempted to kiss away her frustrated tears, but he wouldn't dare be so bold. "I…I want to talk to you."

"Why? Don't you see that I've already ruined everything? I don't deserve your friendship, Joe," Anna cried, turning away from him.

He stepped in front of her and lifted her chin. He gazed into her forlorn eyes. "Don't you dare say that! Do you think I've forgotten how you came and brought Harv and I lunch every day when we were living on the streets? Did you forget that you gave us your father's clothes to wear and brought us into your home and gave us shelter? If anyone is unworthy, it is me."

Anna shook her head in denial. "I kicked you out of my home when you were trying to save it!"

"None of that matters to me."

She stood speechless, eyeing Joe in wonder.

"Anna, will you come meet my folks?" Joe yearned to share so many things with her.

She shrugged in defeat. "Okay."

He reached for her hand and she allowed him to grasp it. It seemed she'd relaxed a little by the time they reached the house. He quickly spotted his parents as they spoke with the bishop. "Anna, this is my mother, Bernice. And my father, Felix."

Anna held her hand out. "Nice to meet you. I'm Anna."

"We've heard a lot about you," Bernice smiled.

Anna briefly smiled at Joseph.

Joseph's father spoke up. "We'd hoped to convince Joseph to come home with us to Ohio."

Anna frowned. "Ohio?" She looked to Joe for confirmation.

"I said I didn't know. It all depends," Joe said.

"On what?" Anna asked.

Joe lifted a brow. "Not, on what. On whom?"

Anna's brow furrowed.

"Anna, will you marry me?"

"You…you want to marry *me*? Why?" Anna's eyes widened before they filled with tears.

Joseph smiled and shrugged. "Because I love you."

THIRTY

*J*oseph glanced up at the judge, then studied Aaron. "Your Honor, I've had many instances in my life where others' choices have affected me. Sometimes we don't know which choice to make, and at other times the correct choice is clear. And although Aaron has sought to bring me harm, I choose to forgive him."

"Do you suggest we let him go free, Sir?" The judge raised his brow.

"*Nee,* he cannot handle freedom. I suggest community service...to the homeless. Your Honor, God showed me a verse from the Bible but I never really understood it. It is this: *He hath shewed thee, O man, what is good; and what doth the LORD require of thee, but to do justly, and to love mercy, and to walk humbly with thy God?* I'd thought, *How can we reconcile justice and mercy? How can the two coincide? Is it possible to do justly and love mercy at the same time?* I think we can offer both justice and mercy."

The judge's eyes lit up. "I have the perfect solution!" His gaze moved from Joseph and settled on Aaron. "Aaron Gingerich."

Aaron glowered at Joe, but looked to the judge. "Yes, Your Honor?"

"I'm sentencing you to six months of permanent community service. You will live in the shelter at the local rescue mission. You will serve those less fortunate in the soup kitchen. You will learn compassion for your fellow man." The judge laced his fingers together. "And if you don't, I have a feeling I'll be seeing you inside my courtroom again."

Aaron nodded silently.

The judge pounded his gavel on the sounding block to dismiss the court.

Anna and Joseph exited the courtroom walking hand in hand.

"I do feel sorry for Aaron, though," Joe said.

"You do?" Anna raised a brow.

"He didn't get you. All that scheming and underhandedness and he still didn't get his prize."

"Oh, so I'm a prize, huh?" Anna smiled up at Joe.

"Oh yes, you are most definitely a prize." He bent down to meet her lips with his.

"Will you two love birds quit all that smoochin' and get on with it? Rachel and *Mammi* put on a fine smellin' roast this mornin' and I'm achin' to give it a try."

"We're coming, Harv. Just hold your horses." Joe smiled at Anna and released her from his embrace.

"Miss Anna, you think you'll be makin' any more of them whoopie pies again? Joe's got me addicted to those things."

Joe perked up. "Isn't God good, Harv?"

"That's what I been tryin' to tell ya all along!" He turned to Anna. "He *finally* gets it." Harvey continued, "Now remember, just because your life seems all fine and dandy and perfect right now, doesn't mean it's always gonna be that way. 'Course, I reckon you know that already. Just don't forget that God is there and He loves ya just as much in the bad times as He does the good. You can always trust God to know what He's doin'."

"Thanks for the reminder, Harv."

"Well, hey. That's what friends are for, *jah?*"

"*Jah.* And a wonderful friend you are."

"Thank you for coming to my little Christmas party." Linda smiled at her friends. "It's not much, but I wanted to have an opportunity to let you know how much you all mean to me. Even though we see each other nearly every day, and I might not always show it, I want to let you know that I love and appreciate you, and I consider you some of my dearest friends."

Anna, Joe, Harv, and *Mammi* all nodded their appreciation and returned her sentiments.

"I do have a small gift for each of you," Linda said, handing each of them a card. She smiled at her husband next to her, at the table she'd set for her guests.

Harvey's face lit up as he opened his gift. "A gift card for a restaurant! Don't go to those too often anymore. What a lovely surprise. Linda, you are a woman after my own heart." He turned to *Mammi* and winked. "Now, if I can just find me a date for dinner, I say I'd be the most happiest man on earth."

Mammi cheeks flamed and she ducked her head.

Joe gave Harv a little kick under the table for embarrassing her.

"Ouch!" Harv bellowed.

"I'm afraid that's not possible, but you may be able to come in a close second." Joe smiled at Anna. His eyes lit up and he remembered his gift for her. Joseph walked over to the counter and pulled out a wrapped box.

Anna's countenance illuminated. "Joe, you didn't have to." She received the gift from his hands and gingerly opened the box. "You bought me the big candle?" Her mouth hung open.

"I saw you looking at it the day we met." He grinned. "Do you like it?"

Anna leaned over and kissed his cheek. "*Denki*, I love it."

Anna handed a gift to Harvey.

Harvey opened the box and hooted. "Why Anna! You went and got me steel-toed boots. The Good Lord knows I need them when I'm around Joe. I think I'll put 'em on right now. "

The group laughed and continued to share in the joy of the season. Harvey read the true Christmas story found in God's Word, and even though the occasion was solemn, they couldn't help but burst into laughter when Harv called the wise men with the three gifts Shadrach, Meshach, and Abednego.

As they sang O Holy Night, Anna shed tears of joy for *Der Herr's* wonderful love for mankind. She marveled at how the God of the universe would even take notice of insignificant mankind. But to God, mankind is not insignificant, they are His beloved creation, whom He sent His Son to die for, so that they might live with Him eternally.

EPILOGUE

*J*oseph Bender raised his head, contemplating the implications of his actions. *Am I really saved?* According to the words he read this morning in God's Holy Word, the answer was yes. He glanced around at the excited countenances of his family and friends and realized how blessed he was.

Today held special meaning. Not only would he be identifying with Christ in baptism and joining the church, but he'd also have the privilege of hearing the announcement of his and Anna's upcoming wedding.

Joseph released a contented sigh. He looked to the women's side of the room and noticed the happy tears that trailed his mother's rejuvenated appearance. He'd like to embrace his mother, but he knew now was not the proper time. Bishop Hostettler would be reading his name to call him forward and ask about his profession of faith. He glanced to his right and brightened as he noticed his father's look of acceptance and approval.

He wore his *for gut* clothes today. Ones that Anna had lovingly sewn for him. He caught her eye and she smiled back, her gaze communicating her love and admiration. In just a few short months, he'd found everything that he would forever hold dear.

Joseph knew he'd cherish God's blessings for as long as he lived.

The End

A LETTER FROM THE AUTHOR

Dear Reader,

I hope you enjoyed reading A Secret Encounter! I'd love to hear your thoughts on the book. Did you have a favorite character? Was there any part that stood out to you in particular? Did the book touch your heart in a special way? Let me know at jebspredemann@gmail.com or visit our Facebook page at www.facebook.com/jebspredemann. We have GIVEAWAYS often, so be sure to check it out!

*A Secret Encounter is a work of fiction, but there are many aspects of the book that are derived from true stories. 'Joe', the hero of A Secret Encounter, along with **Project: Vagabond** (described below), was inspired by a real encounter. One day, while out shopping, I saw a young homeless man (whom Joe is an exact description of) in the parking lot of the grocery store. I thought that I would quickly run into the store, purchase something for the man to eat, give it to him, and while he was eating I would go purchase some clothing for him (he was in desperate need of it). I hadn't been in the store long, but when I came out, he was gone. I drove around the parking lot and surrounding area in hopes of finding him, but he had vanished. I wanted to cry because this man genuinely needed help.*

*This presented a question in my mind: what could I have done differently? The conclusion I came to: **Project: Vagabond**.*

What if I'd had something in the car already? What if I'd been prepared? A couple of quotes come to mind: He who fails to plan, plans to fail. And Where there is no vision, the people perish. *If I'd been prepared, I could have given 'Joe' something to eat and drink. I could have given him the Gospel – a chance at a new life. I could have offered him hope and encouragement.*

Instead, I offered him nothing. NOTHING!

Despite all of that, I think God had it planned that way to open my eyes. To give me a vision, a plan, a purpose. Before I left the parking lot that day, God placed the idea for this book in my mind. It has been a burden on my heart. A burden and a blessing.

One of my children asked if I thought that perhaps 'Joe' was an angel in disguise. I thought of the verse from Hebrews, Be not forgetful to entertain strangers: for thereby some have entertained angels unawares. *I don't know if 'Joe' was an angel or not. Most likely not, but you never know.*

*I'm hoping that you, yes YOU, will become a part of **Project: Vagabond**. Perhaps you can print the last pages of this book and share it with those in your church: a women's group, a youth group, or simply share it with your pastor. There is a special offer for those who sign up for **Project: Vagabond**. Not a bribe or anything, but my way of saying 'thank you'. (Read **Project: Vagabond** page below for details.)*

Another issue this book tackles is sexual abuse. Because this is such a sensitive subject, I did not delve into it deeply. Does this kind of thing happen in Amish communities? Unfortunately, it does. 'Mary' was taken from a true story as well.

While the Amish are generally an upright People, they are human – and thus sinful – as well. There are wicked/depraved souls in every people group and the Amish are no exception.

Fortunately, God offers His love, healing, and forgiveness to all. And we can take comfort in the fact that God is the Righteous Judge. There is nothing that happens that He does not see. We have God's Word on it, that someday He will destroy all wickedness, depravity, and sin. We must trust Him on this.

And we must trust Him with our very lives as well. God is a Father to the Fatherless, He is our Blessed Hope, our Righteousness, the Way, the Truth, and the Life, and the only way to Heaven. John 3:16-18 says, For God so loved the world, that he gave his only begotten Son, that whosoever believeth in him should not perish, but have everlasting life. For God sent not his Son into the world to condemn the world; but that the world through him might be saved. He that believeth on him is not condemned: but he that believeth not is condemned already, because he hath not believed in the name of the only begotten Son of God.

Lastly, I'd like to say thank you. Thank you for investing your time and intellect in this book. I hope it met or exceeded your expectations. Above all, I hope it was a blessing to you and touched your heart in a significant way. If you wouldn't mind, it would be a wonderful blessing if you would leave a review or tell someone about this book. Denki*!*

Blessings,
J. Spredemann
(Rom.10:9-13 KJV)

Please see Project: Vagabond information below!

PROJECT: VAGABOND

*"...Lord, when saw we thee an hungered, and
fed thee? or thirsty, and gave thee drink?...Inasmuch
as ye have done it unto one of the least of these my
brethren, ye have done it unto me."*

Matthew 25:37, 40

Q. **What is Project: Vagabond?**

A. Project: Vagabond is essentially God's love in action. It is
a network of compassionate individuals who want to see their
cities impacted for the cause of Christ.

Q. **What does Project: Vagabond do?**

A. The premise is simple, really. Buy items to help those less
fortunate. We place these items in a simple brown paper lunch
sack and keep them in a designated area in our vehicle: i.e.
box, basket. When we encounter someone who looks like they
could use a helping hand (think 'Will work for food') we give
them a bag and let them know that Jesus loves them. *Please
use caution here – not all people will be like Joe and Harv in *A
Secret Encounter*!

Q. **What's in the bag?**

A. In our bags, we place a bottle of water, a small bag of pretzels (or other snack), applesauce (or cup of fruit), a small KJV New Testament (we purchase these from Dollar Tree), and a Gospel tract. It's not much, but it's enough to show someone you care. We have the children color on the bags and write 'Jesus loves you' or another special message on them. This involves the children and teaches them social responsibility and compassion. They can also help fill the bags.

Q. **How can I get involved?**

A. This can either be an individual project or you can solicit help from those in your church. Since this premise is so simple and takes little effort, you may be surprised how many volunteer to help. Maybe this can be a once a month project for your youth ministry.

Q. **What do I need?**

A. Compassion and a desire to see souls reached for Christ. But practically speaking, you'll need the following items:

- A plastic box, a basket, or some other container that will hold a few paper lunch sacks.
- Paper lunch sacks
- Bottled water

- Individualized snacks (pretzels, applesauce, granola bars, crackers, etc.) We strive to include healthier snacks.
- Bibles
- Gospel tracts (order free from http://www. fellowshiptractleague.org/)

Other than the tracts, all of these items can be purchased at your local Dollar Tree or online at www.dollartree.com!

This page may be copied, printed, and distributed for those participating in Project: Vagabond. Upon signing up for Project: Vagabond, contact the author via www.jebspredemann.com and receive a special code to download the book A Secret Encounter for FREE

A Secret of the Heart

J.E.B. Spredemann

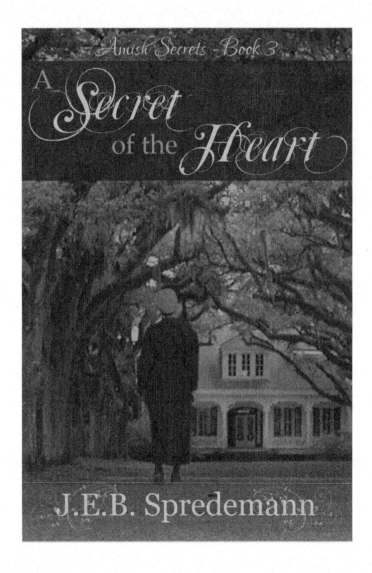

Lillianna Zook and Thomas Girod had been secret friends throughout most of their Amish childhood, but they part ways when Lillianna's family moves to a district in another state. She fears their friendship has been lost forever until a chance encounter brings them in contact once again. Lillianna learns that Thomas needs money – a lot of it – and it's a matter of life and death. Lillianna is willing to do anything she can to help Thomas, so when an opportunity arises where she can make a lot of money in a short time, she doesn't hesitate. But will her sacrifice be worth the trials this new opportunity presents?

Available in online bookstores Fall 2014

Introducing:

Amish Fairly Tales
CINDY'S STORY

*Cindy escapes her harsh reality
by pretending to be someone she isn't...*

PROLOGUE

Ella stood near her father's grave. *He's really gone.* Tears welled in her eyes and dripped onto the ribbon of her prayer *kapp* as she thought of *Mamm*'s funeral several years earlier. She'd been just three then, but she still remembered *Mamm's* beautiful smile and kind words. Although her father had remarried, the gaping hole left by her mother's death had never been filled.

A cold hand on her arm demanded her attention. *"Mother said we need to go now,"* her stepsister Priscilla said in Pennsylvania Dutch.

Ella nodded and brushed her tears away. She followed Priscilla to the family buggy and stared out at the gray sky as she, her stepmother, and two older stepsisters traveled toward home. The clip-clop of the horse's hooves didn't soothe her the way they usually did.

"We are moving tomorrow," Mother Clara declared. "I have no need of this large farm and with no man around, we won't be able to keep up with it. I've already accepted an offer which is more than generous. We will be able to buy something much smaller that will suit our needs."

Nine-year-old Matilda bounced excitedly. "Where will we move, *Mamm*?"

"I thought Indiana might be a nice place. Since it's so cold up north, I plan to join one of the smaller settlements in the south," she answered satisfactorily.

"But I'd have to leave *Dat* and *Mamm*," Ella worried aloud.

Mother Clara squeezed her hand tightly and Ella winced. "We won't have any bad attitudes about this. Do you hear me, Ella? Your parents are dead now. You can stop your nonsense."

Ella nodded silently as moisture gathered in the corners of her eyes.

"*Gut*. Girls, you must begin packing immediately. Ella, you will tend to the animals. You may eat your supper when the chores are completed."

Ella wanted to protest and ask when she would have time to pack up *her* things, but she wouldn't risk more of her stepmother's reproof. She guessed she'd be packing while the rest of the house slept in peace. Just as long as she could take her *Mamm's* special chest with her. Right now, that's all that mattered.

CHAPTER 1

Ten years later...

"*Donner wetter!* You *ferhoodled* horse – get back here!" Nathaniel called out. He leaped onto Winsome's back and charged after the wild steed. "Go get him, girl."

Nat watched in dismay from atop Winsome as the white stallion jumped their pasture fence and raced down the lane. If he didn't reach him before he reached the main highway...

He wouldn't allow his thoughts to ponder that possibility. Besides, that was several miles away. Surely the horse would be in his secure grasp long before then. He hoped... and prayed.

"Whoa! Whoa!" Nathaniel called out to the new horse. Winsome began to slow down. "No, not you girl!" He squeezed his thighs, urging his horse to continue forward. "I knew I should have kept Bishop in his pen. Stupid dog," he uttered under his breath.

"Prince, you've got to slow down!" he hollered as he watched the frightened horse fade from his view. *God, I need your help. You've got to stop that horse...*

Available NOW at participating online bookstores!

CPSIA information can be obtained
at www.ICGtesting.com
Printed in the USA
BVOW03s1016010217
475030BV00002B/115/P